EAST GRAND LAKE

UNIVERSITY OF CALGARY
Press

EAST GRAND LAKE

TIM RYAN

Brave & Brilliant Series

ISSN 2371-7238 (Print) ISSN 2371-7246 (Online)

University of Calgary Press
2500 University Drive NW
Calgary, Alberta
Canada T2N 1N4
press.ucalgary.ca

LIBRARY AND ARCHIVES CANADA CATALOGUING IN PUBLICATION

Title: East Grand Lake / Tim Ryan.
Names: Ryan, Tim (Short story writer), author.
Series: Brave & brilliant series ; 31.
Description: Series statement: Brave & brilliant series ; 31 | A novel in fourteen stories.
Identifiers: Canadiana (print) 20220490201 | Canadiana (ebook) 2022049021X | ISBN
    9781773854441 (hardcover) | ISBN 9781773854458 (softcover) | ISBN 9781773854465 (PDF)
    | ISBN 9781773854472 (EPUB)
Classification: LCC PS8635.Y3589 E27 2023 | DDC C813/.6—dc23

The University of Calgary Press acknowledges the support of the Government of Alberta through the Alberta Media Fund for our publications. We acknowledge the financial support of the Government of Canada. We acknowledge the financial support of the Canada Council for the Arts for our publishing program.

Printed and bound in Canada by Marquis
This book is printed on Enviro Book Natural paper

Editing by Aritha van Herk
Copyediting by Naomi K. Lewis
Cover art: Colourbox 41968712
Cover design, page design, and typesetting by Melina Cusano

For Stacy and Maura

"Nineteen seventy-two will be the longest year thus far in the history of recorded time—the longest by all of two seconds."

New York Times, December 28, 1972

"I've been waiting a long time for last year. But I guess it's just not coming again."

Now Wait For Last Year, Philip K. Dick

SHAYNE

Two seconds.

That's what Mr. Burns told us in the last science class of the year. He told us the year would have two seconds more than any other year in history.

"The longest year ever," he told us.

I already knew that.

The conversation with Mom at breakfast went like this:

"I think we could all use a change of scenery. A trip to the Camp sounds fun, doesn't it?"

"No," I answered.

"You'll get to see all your cousins and uncles and aunts."

"I don't know those people."

"You do, too."

"No, I don't."

"Well, they like you."

"How can they like me if they don't know me?"

"Well, they will."

"Why?"

"Everybody likes you."

"No, they don't."

"What about all your friends at school."

"I don't have any friends at school."

"Sure, you do!"

"I keep telling you, I don't."

"What about that Tony?"

"Who's Tony?"

The Camp is this place my mom's family, the Murphys, have on East Grand Lake. It's not a 'camp' in the sense of tents, cooking fires, and sleeping bags. It's a cottage. No idea why they call it the Camp. Mom talked a lot about the Camp as the summer approached. I knew it was important to her that we go.

If it were any other year, I would have put up a huge stink.

Mom packed snacks, sleeping bags, and music. We dropped the cat off with an old lady whose house smelled like Vicks mixed with baby powder—I felt almost as sorry for the cat as I did for myself.

After a stop at 7/Eleven for Slurpees, we drove down the 401 out of the city, past where the zoo's getting built, the crazy-looking nuclear reactors, and the giant car factories. After Oshawa, it was mainly farmers' fields, ponds, and patchy forests.

In the back of the station wagon, Emm and I spread out sleeping bags to lie with our heads up against the rear gate. Because the window slanted inwards slightly, we could look straight up into the sky. We counted airplanes and birds and clouds that looked like fish. When we got bored with that, we played punch buggy, but Emm kept getting distracted and I kept getting to punch her. When she got tired of being punched, we pulled out the Lego. We made a skate park with little Lego boarder-dudes who did tricks on the rails and stuff. Sometimes the car lurched left or right, flinging the Lego pieces into a window. When that happened, we pretended it was an earthquake and the Lego dudes needed help.

"Waaa Oooo! Waaa Oooo!" Emm was the police.

I slapped my chest for the helicopter.

We drove for days. We counted the mileage signs, slept all together in king-sized motel beds, stopped at gas station toilets, and survived car sickness. I didn't have to deal with school, or neighbours bringing over gross casseroles, or priests coming around, interrupting my TV shows to 'talk to the family.' In the car, it was the three of us, the passing scenery, Mom's music, and the engine's hum.

The world felt almost normal again.

On the third day, about an hour after dinner from a roadside canteen—I got fried clams, French fries, and a root beer—Mom turned off the asphalt onto a dirt road that disappeared into a forest. The road had these huge craters, and even though Mom drove slowly, we got bounced all over the place in the back of the station wagon. Emm laughed hard enough that the juice she was drinking came out her nose, making me laugh even harder. We bumped along the road through trees for what seemed like forever, until the branches parted, and we coasted into a clearing.

Mom whooped, "We're here!" made a sharp right, stopped the car in the middle of a giant mud puddle, and honked the horn.

It looked like one of those places you see in horror films, where bad stuff happens but no one is smart enough to leave. A squat brown cottage with yellow trim sat between our car and a lake. The cottage had a metal roof, a rooster weathervane, and a row of windows that looked into a kitchen. A smaller cabin, painted the same colour as the cottage, sat in the middle of a huge lawn on the other side of our car. Beside the cabin, there was this tiny golf course that for some dumb reason had sand around the holes instead of grass. Beyond the golf course I could see a vegetable garden and then the forest we had driven through. At the side of the cabin was what looked like—

"An outhouse?" I panicked.

Mom laughed. "It used to be. It's a tool shed now."

I calmed down a bit, but still felt anxious about this weird, backwoods place. A bunch of barefoot, dirty kids in swimsuits appeared from the trees and paths around us. As they approached the car, I told myself it was likely Mom's honk that brought them, but the way they all came at the same time, staring at us in the car, I couldn't stop thinking I might be in a horror movie. As I told myself that they were only kids, adults started showing up, and suddenly there were like twenty people I didn't know outside our car. My chest got tight, hard to breathe. My hands got sweaty. I slid down my seat.

Mom stepped out of the car, stretched, and went over to the adults. Emm jumped through the back window onto the dirt road, super excited—like every eight-year-old is about everything—and started talking to the kids. I was left alone, unsure about who these people were, where I was, and why. Home seemed a long way away.

Mom eventually noticed me still in the car. She came over and leaned through the open window. "Are you coming out?"

"No."

"These are your cousins."

"I told you already, I don't know any of them."

"Sure, you do. You met them that Thanksgiving in Kingston."

I had no idea what she was talking about.

"You remember. The year after Emm was born?"

I wanted to point out that was seven years ago, but then the crowd parted, and an old guy moseyed up to us from the stone path beside the cottage.

"Dad!" Mom shouted and ran over to hug him.

Everyone calls my grandpa 'the Doctor,' because he's the doctor in the town Mom grew up in. He gave Mom a kiss, Emm a big hug, and waved at me with a smile. He pulled Mom over to a stand of spruce trees that divided the cottage from the neighbour's place. They talked for a while. I couldn't hear them from the car, but Mom looked over at me a few times. I knew who they were talking about.

While they talked, the rest of the crowd disappeared down the stone path toward the lake, including Emm. I started to feel the tightness leave me.

When they finally stopped talking, the Doctor looked at me, winked, put his arm around Mom's shoulders, and led her toward the cottage. Mom kept looking back at me as she was gently pulled inside.

Alone at last, I climb into the back of the station wagon, where I sit in the stillness on my sleeping bag and think. After I sit for a bit, I figure it'll help me calm down to do something. I dismantle the Lego skateboard park and try to build the cottage I see out the side window. I have half a bottle of root beer left from dinner and a fistful of salt and vinegar chips from when we stopped for lunch. With the snack and the Lego and no one around, I'm doing okay. I start building the cottage base, making it square and even. The brown and yellow Lego bricks are almost the same colour as the cottage. When I run out of brown Lego bricks, I have to use red ones, but it still looks okay.

It takes me a long time to build the walls and windows, but eventually I start building the roof. As I do, the Doctor comes out of the cottage, alone.

I figure he's gonna to try to talk me into getting out of the car to join everyone. Instead, he goes in and out of the cottage, bringing out a chair, then an easel, then a big canvas. He puts the canvas—with a half-painted picture of the cottage—on the easel and a wooden box on the chair. He stands behind the chair and looks at the cottage. He adjusts the easel slightly, then goes back inside. After a few minutes, he comes back holding a mug of what I assume is coffee, and an ashtray. He tugs a small yellow table across the grass to the chair and balances the mug and ashtray on it. He stands behind the chair again, pulls a pack of cigarettes from his shorts pocket, lights one, and gives it an absent-minded puff as he faces the cottage, head tilted. After a few more puffs on the cigarette, he takes paints, brushes, and a palette out of the wooden box and places them on the table.

Small, skinny, deeply tanned, the Doctor holds his paintbrush in one hand, cigarette in the other. He doesn't flick the cigarette, letting the cylinder of ash get longer and longer as he paints. Eventually, the ash is longer than the rest of the cigarette. It's kind of freaky how the ash clings, defying gravity. Every now and then, he rests the cigarette in the ashtray beside his paints to lift the mug shakily into the air. The first couple of times he does this, I'm sure the coffee's gonna slosh, stain his cream tennis shorts, and scald the old guy. But after each slurp, he flutters the mug back to its saucer, then gets back to his painting.

He uses some kind of knife to spread blue-grey paint across the top of the picture, humming or singing to himself the whole time. His shakes disappear when he paints. At one point, he grabs a tube of yellow paint and squeezes a coil onto the wood palette. The paint is the consistency of toothpaste, nothing like the watery stuff we use at school.

"You're Shayne?" he asks suddenly without looking in my direction.

I almost choke on a sip of root beer. "Uh, yeah."

"I'm your grandfather, most people call me the Doctor."

I already know that, but I figure I should be nice. I say, "Hi."

"Welcome to Grand Lake."

"Thanks." I'm a little suspicious about where this conversation might go, but he doesn't seem to be interested in getting me out of the car.

He goes back to painting the roof of the cottage. It's aluminum, so he adds white, then grey and some light blue to get the colour right. Honestly, he's no Michelangelo, but at least I can tell what he's painting. I guess he's okay.

I'm trying to finish the roof of my structure, but it's hard to make the rooster weathervane out of Lego. I get absorbed and forget he's out there until I hear him say, "Well, that's enough for today."

He starts folding up his chair and stuffing the paints back into their box. He sings that song about a kid—I always picture a kid—who finds a box on a beach that he takes and then can't get rid of. I know it from summer camp.

The kid with the box I totally understand. There's lots of times you think something is great, and then you show someone else, and they think it's stupid, then you think it must be stupid, too. Or you figure out later, after you've spent time with whatever it is, that maybe it isn't what you thought it was. The problem is, by then, you've told everyone else how great the box is, and it's hard to go back and admit that maybe you made a mistake. Then you're sort of stuck with the box, even though you know it isn't what you thought it was, unless you're willing to admit to everyone else that you were wrong. And that's hard to do—admit you were wrong—after you've been bragging about the box.

I get the kid in the song. If it's a kid.

The Doctor wipes his hands in a rag he takes from the paintbox. He starts to take the canvas off the easel when I see that he forgot to include what I was working on.

"You forgot the weathervane." I point to his picture.

He looks at his picture then up at the roof.

"You're right." He laughs. "I did." He turns to look at me. "Good thing someone's paying attention. I'll make a note for next time."

It's starting to get dark, and I can see the moon peeking through the sky.

"Everything all right in there?" he asks.

He asks like he's interested in the answer. Not like he thinks I'm stupid staying in the car when everyone else is doing stuff. He's checking on me, like a grandpa would, or at least should, but he's not all judgy when he does it.

"Yeah, I'm good."

Then he says something my mom would never say. "I bet it's nice and quiet in there, eh?"

I nod.

"Are you going to sleep there tonight?"

I nod again, expecting him to try to convince me that it's not such a great idea.

But he asks, "Need anything?"

"Nah, I'm good."

"How about a pillow?"

It's a good idea. Emm and I used rolled-up sweatshirts for our heads during the drive here, but a rolled-up sweater isn't as good as a real pillow.

"A pillow'd be great. Thanks."

"Is it okay if I tell your mom that you're going to sleep in the car tonight?"

He looks at me like if I said no, he wouldn't say anything. This sort of surprises me. Lots of adults—teachers, priests, parents—ask you if it's okay to tell so-and-so, like they're trying to respect your privacy, but you know they're going to tell anyway. They're just trying to feel less guilty about blabbing your secret stuff to other people. In the end, though, they don't feel that guilty, and your permission isn't going to change what most of them do.

He adds, "That way she won't worry about you."

Even his reason is different than most people. In my experience, most people want to talk about others to show how much they know. Like they have access to this big secret and they're granting some giant favour to the person they tell it to, when all along they were going to tell anyway, because it makes them feel important. The telling doesn't really have anything to do with passing along information, it's more like bragging. I hate that.

I think about what he says for a second, but because he gives me the impression that he will only tell if I say he can, it somehow makes it easier for me to agree.

"Sure." I say, like it's no big deal.

"Good. Hopefully, she'll get some sleep, too."

He gathers up his paints box, the easel, and the canvas. Once he figures out how to carry all this stuff, he says, "Okay, then. I'll grab you a pillow and let your mom know." Then he heads into the cottage.

I go back to my Lego cottage to finish the roof. I figure out how to make an okay weathervane. As I make a chimney, a group of kids comes out onto the lawn. I duck, hoping they won't notice me, but I catch a few of them looking in the direction of the car. One little kid even waves. They put a coffee can in the middle of the road, a girl kicks it, and most of the kids scatter.

I've played Kick the Can lots. It's always the same: little kids keep getting caught. They're funny. They know the object of the game is not to get tagged, but they wanna play to kick the can. You know: sprint up to the can, feel your toes crumple the side of the can, hear the can clanging along the ground. That's the whole point of the game for them. Adults always try to explain how it's better to hide or run away, and that way you might not get tagged.

They explain how not worrying about the can is a better way to win the game. But if little kids get to kick the can themselves, in their minds, they've won already. They don't care about hiding, or running away, or being the last one tagged. They just want to kick the can. You gotta admire little kids for that.

Besides, those people who think they know a better way to play usually just get tagged later in the game. They end up tagged, don't win the game, and they don't get to kick the can. Most little kids seem happy to me, but most adults seem worried, or sad, or angry. I bet it comes down to kicking that can and seeing what might happen, not worrying about winning the game. I think that's the way Dad was. He was focussed on kicking the can whenever he could. Sure, maybe he got tagged, and maybe the game ended faster that way, but at least he got to kick the can.

When the game is over, I hear a tap on the window. The Doctor's back. He has a pillow and some other stuff on his arm.

I roll down the window, and he passes me the pillow.

"Here you go. This should make sleeping more comfortable. I also brought you a flashlight, some toilet paper, and my old army canteen, full of water. In case you get thirsty."

"Thanks."

"If you need to use the bathroom, you can come inside or go in the bushes over by the toolshed." He points to the shed I thought was an outhouse when we first got here. "Throw your paper in the garbage cans by the shed and use some of the canteen water to wash your hands. Okay?"

"Uh, okay."

"If you want to clean up now for bed, I can keep lookout for you."

I like to brush my teeth before bed. I don't get a sneaky will-lock-me-out-of-the-car vibe from him. I decide to take him up on his offer. Sure enough, he lets me get out of the car, brush my teeth, and get back in without making a big deal.

"Okay, we're good?" he asks.

"Yeah."

"Well, have a good sleep. I'll see you tomorrow?"

I nod.

"If you want to come inside during the night, there's a couch in the living room with a blanket. Okay?"

"Okay."

"Make sure to close the windows, that way the bugs don't get in."

He doesn't try to convince me to follow him. He walks toward the cottage, waves over his shoulder without looking back, and leaves me alone.

By this time, it's totally dark. I put the Lego cottage on the driver's seat to clear out the back of the station wagon and open my sleeping bag. I give the pillow a fluff, put the canteen in the bucket built into the window ledge, then stretch out in the back of the car.

Through the back window I can see the tops of the trees, the moon, and a bright red dot low in the night sky. I think it might be Mars. There's a ton of stars. I try to figure out as many constellations as I can, like Dad taught me.

Eventually, I hafta pee, so I go in the woods like the Doctor said to. When I get back to the car, I slip into my sleeping bag and use my flashlight to read a few pages of a book, but my eyes get heavy. I turn off the light.

In no time, I'm asleep.

SCOTTIE

Scottie wakes in the loft with the sun streaming through the window onto his pillow. He looks out across the backyard into the forest. Down on the lawn are remnants from last night: an inflatable unicorn wrapped in a towel, a beer bottle one of his aunts or uncles had half finished, two floaties, and a small pink shirt spilling out of a shopping bag. A car is parked up by the cabin. Scottie knows Shayne slept there overnight, but he doesn't know why.

It is quiet.

Scottie slips out of bed, pulls on his swim trunks, then tiptoes past his sleeping cousins and down the stairs. In the kitchen, he uses both hands to pour himself a glass from the gallon jug of milk. Eight large glass jars sit on the kitchen counter filled with baked goods and baking supplies. Reaching up on tiptoe, he takes a doughnut from one jar and drops it two jars over into the sugar. He flips the doughnut, then plucks it out, leaving brown doughnut crumbs in the white sugar. He licks his fingers and grabs his milk. Trailing a path of sugar, he heads back through the dining room.

No one is awake yet.

Out the back door, he goes around the picnic table on the lawn—kicking the unicorn as he passes—to the side of the cottage where his towel, damp with dew, hangs over a clothesline. Sunlight reaches through the forest, casting long tree shadows onto the brown sides and yellow trim of the cottage. The air is cool, the sky a cloudless blue.

A sparrow sings from the birch tree over the clothesline where the towels hang. Scottie wonders where sparrows sleep at night. Do they sleep on tree branches? How do they not fall? He would fall if he tried sleeping up on a tree branch. That high up, he'd be too afraid to sleep. Can a bird be afraid of heights? That'd be terrible.

Slinging the towel over his shoulder, he pads barefoot over root, rock, and grass to the old boathouse, now another place to sleep when more cousins come. He slides the large nail on a string out of the metal hasp that fastens the door and steps inside. Four small cots are jammed into the room. One of the cot's covers are flung aside and there's an impression of the sleeper's head in the middle of the pillow. A set of keys dangles on a hook in the wall above this pillow and an open duffle bag sits on the bed across from it. The boathouse has a low ceiling, exposed studs, and stale, damp air. An orange, yellow and brown shag carpet covers the floor. Lake water laps against the big window at the far end of the room.

Scottie finishes his doughnut and wipes his fingers on his swim trunks. He scans the room: a water-basketball net, two fishing rods, a tackle box, three paddles, a yellow plastic raincoat, two winter coats, a sleeping bag, two yellowing pillows, a stack of old newspapers, three mohair blankets, a quilt, a cone of buckets, a football, two oars, an ancient reading lamp, and, hanging on hooks mounted to the walls, lifejackets. Under a pillow on one of the unoccupied cots, he sees the bill of his baseball cap.

He hid here last night during Kick the Can. He would have won the game if Aidan hadn't found him. Scottie lost his cap when he ducked around Aidan and dashed from the boathouse to the backyard, where the empty coffee can sat on the gravel driveway. As he was planting his foot to kick, Connor tagged him. When the game was called, Scottie forgot to go back for his cap. By the time he remembered, it was bedtime, and he was in pajamas.

He puts the cap on, leaves the boathouse, and steps gingerly over the wet grass to the concrete retaining wall. He gazes at the water, the calm lake. He takes a sip of milk and wonders which is colder, the milk or the lake? He turns, places his glass on one arm of a yellow Adirondack chair, drapes his towel over the chair's back, and puts his cap on the seat.

Two concrete steps lead down to the dock. He pauses at the top, surveying the scene—the water, the other cottages dotting the forest, the endless sky.

Yesterday, his older cousins ran down the dock and leapt off the end, high into the air, plummeting in cannonballs, jack-knives, swan dives and one almost-somersault. He sat cross-legged on the retaining wall watching them, unsure.

"Scottie! C'mon!" James yelled as he sailed into the sky.

A little later, his mom came over. "Do you want to try?"

He shrugged her away.

The Doctor came over and squatted beside him, "I could go with you?"

Scottie shook his head.

Then Danny appeared from inside the cottage.

Cousin Danny was almost ten, with freckles all over his face and a scary twinkle in his eye. He had seven brothers and sisters, but Danny liked to stand out. A few days ago, he left his younger sister Marcie stuck up the tallest tree in the forest without telling anyone. She was up there until, at dinner, one of the aunts noticed she was missing. Danny had convinced some of the younger cousins that mud was as good as snow for a fight, and he had snuck one of Grammy's cigarettes up to the fort, then blamed Rory when the adults caught him. Rory hadn't even been to the fort, because Matt wouldn't let him join the club.

"You gonna jump?" Danny asked with his hands on his hips.

Scottie didn't answer.

"It's easy! Look!" Danny ran off the dock and did a cannonball.

When Danny got out of the water, he came over to Scottie. "See? It's fun. Kinda scary, but fun."

Scottie looked Danny in the eye. Danny's eyes weren't like Mom's eyes or the Doctor's—they offered no comfort.

"You can do it," Danny said, but his shoulders, arms, and face said otherwise.

By now, the other cousins were watching.

"Look. I'll even do it with my eyes shut!"

And he did. Danny ran down the dock with his eyes shut and jumped in.

Mac, a neighbour who let Scottie feed ducks from his dock, squatted beside Scottie and said, "Don't mind him. You only go if you want to."

But Danny called from the water, "What're ya, chicken?"

"Stop it!" one of Scottie's cousins warned, but Danny didn't even listen to adults.

"Scaredy cat! Nya! Nya! Look at the scaredy cat!" Danny pointed and turned to the crowd on the lawn, smirking. "Won't even jump in the lake!"

Now the adults noticed.

"That's enough," Uncle Ed, Danny's father, said.

"But he's chicken! Bock! Bock! Deep fried!"

"I said, THAT'S ENOUGH." Ed rose from his seat.

Danny knew he was in for it, but he kept at it. He climbed out of the water and ran down the path beside the cottage, laughing and yelling. "Chicken pants! Scaredy cat! Too scared to jump!" He had an audience and a victim and no one fast enough to catch him.

Scottie stands two paces from the water's edge of the dock. A loon paddles out in the middle of the lake. Black with white markings on its back, the loon is too far away for Scottie to see its eyes. As the loon moves across the water, Scottie calls out "Helloooo!" and waves. His voice echoes around the cove. He thinks the loon stops for an instant and looks his way. Morning allies.

The water off the end of the dock is over his head. He won't hit bottom, but the lake has weeds and clams and leeches and who knows what else. Fish might swim up against him and touch him on the leg or get inside his swim trunks or—hang on! Does anything in the lake bite?

Down through the surface of the water the dock's legs are stuck in the sandy bottom. His uncles put the dock in at the start of the summer using ropes and hammers. He sees a piece of rope connecting one of the legs to a cinder block. Around the cinder block something is moving. Minnows. Minnows are okay. They don't bite or touch or get caught where they aren't supposed to. Minnows scatter when you come near. They are tiny and fast and afraid.

Scottie likes minnows.

He paces off the length of the dock. He counts twelve steps to the water. If he runs there are fewer—ten strides and then jump. If he jumps too soon, he might not clear the end of the dock. He could scrape his back or hit his head. The minnows would scatter; they wouldn't help. He might fall into the water, bleeding. Blood in water brings sharks!

Wait. Sharks are in the ocean.

He takes a deep breath, walks out until he can bend his toes over the edge of the dock. He imagines pushing off, grabbing one shin in a jack-knife, holding his breath and then . . .

He walks back to the Adirondack chair and puts his cap on. He sits in the chair and finishes his milk. Pretending he is undercover, Scottie pulls the brim of his cap down low over his eyes. He peeks out from under to watch the lake. If he were undercover, he would have to write a report. He'd have one of those spiral flip pads and a pencil to make notes. He'd have to swallow his notes if he got caught. That would taste bad.

A ladybug crawls up his towel toward the top of the chair. Scottie watches her steady climb. The towel must seem a lot bigger to the ladybug than the dock seems to him. She isn't afraid. As soon as the ladybug makes it to the top of the chair, he will run and jump off the dock. She climbs slowly. Past an orange stripe and then a white stripe and then another orange stripe. Her legs move quickly. Could his legs move that quickly? If they could, how fast would he go? The ladybug stops. She is almost at the top. Come on ladybug! The ladybug opens her spotted wings and flies away.

That's not fair! She can fly. She didn't get to the top . . . does he still have to jump?

When Danny had gone, the older cousins went back to jumping off the dock. The adults returned to their papers and conversations. Even though he tried to make himself small and quiet, he felt people not looking at him. After a while, he stood and joined the line of cousins waiting to jump from the dock.

"You can do it!" Finn said quietly. "The first time is the hardest. After that it's fun."

Connor agreed, "We were all scared the first time, even Danny."

One by one the kids launched themselves into the lake, until Scottie found himself at the front of the line. He looked at the dock. He looked at the water. His heart pounded and his legs felt like Jell-O. He searched the yard and found his mom.

"C'mon! You can do it!" Mac called from his porch next door. Everyone was looking now.

Then someone clapped. One person's clap turned into two. Two into four. Soon everyone was smiling, clapping rhythmically, encouraging him on.

He stood at the front of the line, unmoving.

The clapping grew louder, then chanting: "Scottie! Scottie! Scottie!"

He knew they were trying to help. They weren't like Danny. They wanted him to jump. He wanted to jump. He did.

He looked at the dock, looked at the water and then looked at everyone clapping and chanting. He saw the line he would run, the edge of the dock and the perfect jack-knife. He imagined the moment when he would break back up through the surface of the lake with his arms raised high.

He crouched and took a big breath.

The clapping seemed to grow louder.

He pictured pushing off, his leap, grabbing one knee, the big splash and then—

He turned, bolted inside, ran up to the loft, jumped into bed, and pulled the covers over his head, hoping no one would follow.

Scottie shivers. In only his trunks, he doesn't have much protection from the morning air—even though they are Batman swim trunks. He pulls himself out of the chair and, with his arms crossed tight against his chest, tiptoes to the steps.

Batman'd run—faster than any of them—jump off—higher than any of them—and do a perfect cannonball into the lake. Scottie flexes his biceps in his best strongman pose, ribs and pelvic bone prominent. His swim trunks slip down his hips. He grabs them.

He makes his way out to the middle of the dock. The minnows are still there. Hundreds of tiny black and silver fish. Now they are floating a few inches below the surface. What are they doing anyway? Eating? Sleeping? Every few seconds one darts ahead of the group or school or whatever a bunch of minnows is called.

Do you call a bunch of minnows a school?

He will ask his teacher when he starts first grade in September. "Hoooloohoohooo!"

The loon is still out there. The loon's call sounds sad, like the loon wants someone to come and play. Finn says there is only one loon to a lake—unless they have a partner or babies. Still, not a lot of company. Scottie wouldn't like to be a loon.

He remembers the cap on his head, turns and frisbees it onto the front lawn. He stands on the dock. He goes up on his toes three times. He bends at the waist and eyes his take-off. Once he has done one, the others will be easy. It's the first one that's a bit scary. Not that he's scared. Being scared is for little kids.

He will count from ten then jump. That way he can't back down. If he starts at ten, he'll jump when he gets to zero. That'll make it official, and he'll know exactly when to jump. Once he starts the count there isn't anything he can do. He'll have to jump.

He takes a big breath in. He thinks 'Ten!'

Behind him, the window blinds go up. He turns to look and Grammy waves at him through the window. Scottie waves back.

It's not his fault she interrupts him. He was going to go.

Grammy points to the plate she holds.

Breakfast? If there's bacon, it'll get eaten first.

He looks out at the loon, waiting for him. It probably already had breakfast. It's easy to swim, once you've had breakfast. The water isn't as cold with a full stomach. You float better if your belly's full . . . at least you might.

Scottie runs to the door. He'll have breakfast first.

After a good breakfast he'll jump.

He knows he will.

SHAYNE: SCOTTIE AND BETSY

I wake up to fogged windows. I have no idea what time it is, but it feels early. It's musty and humid in the car, like a locker room after a hockey game. I make a porthole through the fog with the palm of my hand to look outside. The lawn has stuff everywhere: clothes, a beer bottle, dishes, and a blow-up unicorn floatie.

Every time I breathe the porthole fogs up, then I have to wipe it again. This happens until I roll down a window. Forest air wafts in cool and fresh, diluting the sour-stale aroma that has simmered in here all night. I can hear the morning chorus and the wind rustling through the trees. It reminds me of the tree that greets me every morning outside my bedroom window. I miss my room, our house, our street.

If Dad were home, I could have stayed with him. But thinking this wakes that little ball in my chest, the one Dr. Nygaard keeps telling me to befriend. According to him, I'm supposed to counter the ball with gratitude, but it's hard to feel grateful when you're angry with everyone and everything.

Dr. Nygaard's breathing exercises work if I figure out what's happening early enough. The exercises are a distraction, but that's the point: thinking about something else makes the ball shrink. It's better than letting it grow into a wrecking ball that smashes me. Like that hole in the wall I made. It's because I kicked a hole in the wall of the boys' change room that I had to start seeing Dr. Nygaard.

I breathe.

In two-three. Out two-three. In two-three.

From the backdoor, a blonde kid walks onto the lawn, he's maybe six or seven years old. He walks across the grass, kicks the unicorn, and goes to the far side of the cottage. He's carrying a glass of milk and is eating something he holds in the other hand, but he still manages to hook a towel from the clothesline with his elbow, draping it over his shoulder. Then he disappears down the side of the cottage toward the lake.

I find a blueberry muffin in our bag of food, the last of the dozen Mom baked for our trip. She does stuff like that. For Thanksgiving, she makes the turkey and the gravy and the potatoes and everything herself. She makes spaghetti sauce, and we never have pizzas from the restaurant, because Mom makes them for us. If people come over, she spends the whole day making dips and cakes and cookies. If we go over to someone's house for dinner, she ends up bringing half the stuff we eat there. The day before we left to come here, she was in the kitchen all day. I helped make the chocolate chip cookies because I like to eat the dough between dolloping spoonfuls onto the baking sheet. Emm made the muffins. Our kitchen was a mess. I had to dry dishes for an hour after all the baking was done, but we did have good snacks for the trip.

As I'm eating, I think about those two extra seconds we have this year. Mr. Burns said that scientists add it to the world clock. But where do the scientists get those seconds? Do they make time? And if they can make time, can they push time around in other ways? Can they make time go backwards? I wish time could go backwards.

Grammy comes into the kitchen holding a cigarette. She puts a pot of coffee on the stove, then stands smoking at the kitchen sink for a while. She smokes a lot, according to Mom, like the Doctor. No one smokes in our house anymore. When Grammy's done smoking, she starts moving back and forth through the kitchen. She butters some toast, shuffles to the far end of the room, and comes back with a mug. She pours herself a coffee, then leaves the kitchen.

I ask myself if I'd truly like time to go backwards. To see him again. Maybe ask him some questions that are bugging me. When I think about it though, if time goes backwards, then he's still around. If he's still around, then I don't have any of these questions. Maybe going back doesn't matter. It wouldn't change anything. Scientists may be able to make this the longest year, but some parts of time they can't fix.

I grab the canteen and my toothbrush, leave the car, and stand beside the toolshed, where I clean my teeth, splash some of the canteen water on my face, and take a leak.

Behind the shed is a patch of grass and wildflowers over which skips a green and yellow hummingbird. Sometimes the bird stops, hovers, and sticks his tongue down into the flower. He might be drinking. Or eating something? I've never seen a real-life hummingbird before. I watch him bop from flower to flower to flower and then zip away. He reminds me of a bumblebee looking for pollen. Maybe that's what he's doing?

I wipe my face on one of the towels hanging from the clothesline tied between the shed and a tree. There are clotheslines everywhere, all full, which reminds me of how many people are here at the Camp. I get back in the car and finish my muffin, wishing I had something other than water to drink. There's no more movement inside the cottage. I figure most people are still asleep.

I grab a couple of comic books from my backpack and lie on top of my sleeping bag.

It's not like I'm in a rush.

THE LETTER

The red door at the far corner of the living room swings open, and a small woman in curlers shuffles out, a lit cigarette dangling between her right index and middle fingers. Betsy wears a purple silk nightgown, fuzzy red slippers faded from years of use, and a mint-green terry cloth housecoat, its belt, attached through only one of the belt-loops, dragging behind her. Cigarette smoke crawls over the deep wrinkles at the side of her cheeks and eyes, past her brow and through the curlers, before floating into the vaulted space above her head. The ceiling fan disperses the smoke past cloth pennants tacked to the plywood wall memorializing trips to places like San Francisco, Portland, the Alamo, Bar Harbor, and St. Andrews by-the-Sea. As she sweeps through the room, a trickle of ash falls on the black, green, and white carpet chosen years ago to mask the wear of daily life.

Entering the galley kitchen, Betsy removes a metal three-stage coffee maker from the stovetop, popping off the top stage. She adds eight heaping spoonfuls of ground coffee to the filter and clicks the top back onto the pot. She starts the kettle. Gazing out of the kitchen windows across the backyard, she squints to see if Shayne—her grandson who chose to spend the night in the station wagon parked across the lawn—is still in the car. She puffs her cigarette. Her left fingers absentmindedly explore the nest of curlers on her head. Sunlight streams through the halo of smoke above her. When the kettle boils, she pours the water into the top of the coffee pot. The trickle of water and the aroma of coffee flavour the silence.

When the drip stops, she flicks the butt of her cigarette into the large Chock-Full O' Nuts coffee can beside the sink, then sets the pot over low heat on the stove. She opens one of the glass jars sitting on the counter, reaches in, and pulls out a homemade molasses-ginger cookie, which she places on a cutting block built into the counter. From inside one cupboard, Betsy pulls down a dish containing a pat of butter surrounded by congealed fat. She spreads a layer of butter on the flat bottom of the cookie and places it on a paper towel, butter-side up. She digs a faded Maxwell House mug from the metal cupboard, pours herself a coffee and, cradling the paper-towel-wrapped cookie, exits the kitchen.

She moves slowly back to the living room, her too-full coffee dripping onto the carpet. At the far end of the room a large window looks over the front lawn and the lake. A boathouse guards the right side of the lawn, and two silver birch trees curtain the left side. A concrete retaining wall marks the border of the yard with two yellow Adirondack chairs she and Michael bought, years ago, from a toothless Slovakian in his dusty Vermont woodshop on their drive back from a Cape Cod holiday. Scottie, another grandson, sits alone by the lake, playing with his baseball cap.

Betsy rests her mug on the arm of one of the living-room armchairs chairs and with a soft grunt drops into it, cookie held high. Settled, she places the cookie beside the mug and rummages through the pockets of her robe. She extracts a packet of Salem menthol cigarettes and a lighter. These she places on the other arm of the chair. She raises the coffee mug to her lips and takes a cautious sip. Gazing outside at Scottie now standing on the yellow dock, she picks up the cigarette packet and taps the side. As a filter end emerges, she stops, tamps it into the packet, and puts the packet down again. She reaches back into the pocket of her robe and this time pulls out an envelope.

Betsy holds it, crumpled, with fraying corners at the opening end, up to the window as if to ensure it is this envelope she wanted to read and not some other. She then places it on her lap, hand-pressing it over her thigh. She takes another test sip from her coffee and a bite of cookie, leaving a fleck of butter stuck to the fine grey hairs above her lip.

She lifts the flap and pulls out two stationery grade sheets of paper. Unfolding the pages, she reads.

May 1st, 1972

Mom —

Sorry I couldn't talk when you called last week. Sandy Beach dropped into town unexpectedly insisting we go out for seafood. Instead of getting to catch up with you, I spent my evening in downtown Sausalito listening to the musings of Spokane's best-loved news anchor, replete with a hundred observations of how much better the weather was here than there. A year ago, I might have found some excuse to avoid him, but it was a Wednesday, and I was feeling lonely.

You and I haven't talked as much as we should lately, and it's my fault: I haven't had a lot of good news, and I didn't think you needed any more to worry about. The hospital let me go, totally without cause, I should add, and they paid through the nose for it, but it was still a bit unsettling. I'm having some trouble finishing my research without access to a hospital lab and the drug company is giving me a hard time about the advance they gave me. I may have to hire a lawyer.

On another note—and I recognize a letter is a cowardly way to tell you this, but I don't have the energy to tell anyone over the phone—Christine left me for a used car dealer in Ventura, taking Jack with her. Apparently, her church trips up the coast weren't exactly what I imagined them to be. I suppose I should have been suspicious when there were dozens of cars outside the worship hall on the weekends of her so-called retreats. Sometimes it's easier to believe what you want until reality punches you in the gut. By the time you get this, I might be in a better frame of mind to talk about it.

I think about the Camp every day now. The summers we spent there. Fishing, tramping through the woods, waterskiing. Not a care in the world. Sure, a few leeches, but that's not what counted.

Dad taking us to the frog pond, putting on those crazy talent shows, picking berries. I know I can't go back in time, but I like to remember. I keep asking myself, when did life get hard? Probably a stupid question. Maybe it's not life, but the world feels different now.

I've decided to bring Jack to the lake this summer. It's been way too long. He won't even remember the place. He was two years old the last time we came. Maybe we'll head up right after Jack's school is out (Christine wants a pre-honeymoon with the car dealer anyway), but if that timing doesn't work, then for sure in August. It's important to me that Jack gets his chance to see Dad. I'll call with details when I know them.

Sorry again about the other night.

Say hi to everyone.

Love,

Patrick

P.S. Was it me who jumped in the lake first? Or Nellie? We can't agree. Nell claims it was her, but I'm sure it was me. If you know, it will settle a bet.

With a practised hand, Betsy folds the two pages and slides them into the envelope, tucks it back into the pocket of her robe, and takes up the pack of cigarettes, this time withdrawing one. Out the window to her left, one of her grandsons is staring down at the water off the end of the dock, afraid to jump. Out the window through the cottage to her right, another of her grandsons is hiding in a car.

Betsy coughs and, with an almost imperceptible shake of her head, lights the cigarette.

SHAYNE: AIDAN AND CONNOR

In my comic book, Thor's trying to get his hammer back from Loki.

People have started to come outside. I watch two kids playing on the crazy mini golf course. It's not a mini-golf course, more a golf course that's mini. I still haven't figured out why the 'greens' are all sand. Who designed that? I suppose it gives the place a certain character, but it seems kinda stupid if you think about it too much.

A kid about my age trots past the car toward the cottage, holding a bucket. Moments later, the shed door pops open, and a smaller kid falls out onto the grass. He seems disoriented at first. He wipes his eyes as he sits in the middle of the grass, then jumps up and hollers, "Wait for me!" sprinting after the kid with the bucket.

I'm watching these two when a knock on the car window scares the crap out of me.

"Sorry, Shayne." It's Mom. "You okay?"

"Yeah." I say this a little more peevishly than I intended. But to be fair, I don't know why she's sneaking up on me, and it feels like my heart skipped a beat or two.

"Did you sleep?"

"Yeah."

She makes a visor with her hands and peers into the car window. "Do you need to use the bathroom or brush your teeth?"

"I did already." I'm not offering any more information than necessary. I am expecting that anything I say will be used to try and convince me that I should get out of the car.

"Are you going to have some breakfast?"

"I already ate."

Her shoulders slump slightly. "Okay. Well, come join us if you want to."

She's worried. I can tell from the ridges on her forehead. The ridges weren't there a year ago. Her forehead used to be smooth. A year ago, she didn't get headaches every other day. A year ago, she didn't feel the need to come up and hug me every hour. A year ago, she went to work every day and left us with Dad.

A year ago, I wasn't thinking about how different things were a year ago.

The little ball comes back. I'd love to share it with Mom, maybe get her to carry it for a while, but I can't. She has her own ball, and it's a bit much to ask someone to carry two. I keep mine with me, close, near enough that no one else can see it, but it's there if someone looks hard enough. Dr. Nygaard can see it. It makes me angry that the stupid ball is mine with no one to give it to. I'm a kid. Maybe not as small as Emm, but the other kids in my class don't have a little ball. At least I don't think so. Maybe they do. Not the same as mine, but something like it. It's not fair that any of us have these. But it's especially not fair when the one person you thought understood about them decides he's had enough and chucks his ball away for good. When he does that, your ball gets heavier, ridges appear on foreheads, and the inside of a car seems like it might be the only safe place to stay.

"I wanna go home."

She freezes. I think she heard me but isn't sure what to say. She says, "We only just got here."

"So?"

"We're here with family."

"How long?"

"We talked about this. Maybe, two weeks?"

"Two weeks?" Even though I knew this, it still hits me hard when she says it out loud. The ball presses on my chest, growing in weight and density. I can't help it when a tear rolls down my cheek.

"Can I get in the car?" She reaches for the door.

"No! Leave me alone."

"We could talk—"

"GO AWAY!"

She steps back, hands raised in the 'I'm unarmed' pose they do in TV shows.

She watches me through the car window, not coming closer, not saying anything. I'm trying not to look at her, but out of the corner of my eye I can see that she has one hand over her mouth and the other on top of her head. She stands this way for a long time, looking at me through the window, hand over mouth, clearly trying to decide what to do. Why can't she figure it out? It's simple. I told her. She doesn't listen. Or chooses not to. She thinks she knows what I should do, what I want. But she doesn't.

Adults think kids don't *really* know what they want: "You only think you want that." Like somehow adults know what we should want. Every adult I know confuses what they think kids need with what the adult wants the kid to need. Parents say stuff like, 'If only you'd listen to me, you'd be able to do this/not feel that/avoid this.' Like they're experts. As if they didn't go through some or all of what 'kids these days' are struggling with, didn't feel exactly the same way me and all the kids in my school do when stupid adults pretend they 'know better.'

Which they don't.

Not even close.

I'm sure she is about to tell me what she thinks I need to do like she always does, but I'm wrong. She surprises me. Her hands drop to her sides, she smiles at me and says, "Stay there as long as you want, okay? I'm here if you need me. I know it's tough, Shayne. I know you miss him. I do, too. I do. I miss him, and I'm mad at him, and I love him. I'm sorry if this isn't exactly what you wanted. But it's what I think we all need."

I think she's finished, but then she says, "Most of all, I want you to know that I love you." She blows me a kiss and retreats to the cottage.

You gotta hand it to her.

She knows how to make an exit.

BUCKETS

"Aidan! Come on."

"What?" Aidan asks, finishing a shoot-the-moon and pocketing his yo-yo.

Connor doesn't answer, instead strides away across the grass.

Aidan jumps down from the small porch on the front of the cabin. "What are we doing?" he says, jogging after Connor.

"Getting two buckets," Connor says over his shoulder. "I'm checking the shed."

"Oh . . . why?"

"Why what?" Connor answers, jerking open the clasp on the shed door.

"Why are we getting two buckets?"

Prying the door open, Connor answers, "To catch bullfrogs. Why do you think?"

"How would I know?" Aidan mutters under his breath.

"What?"

"Never mind."

Connor disappears into the shed. Aidan wonders where they're going to get the frogs from when a disembodied arm sticks out of the shed door, holding a bucket. "Here, take this."

"Got it," Aidan says.

Connor's arm disappears back into the shed. The scrapes and bangs of his search continue as Aidan waits on the lawn. A robin sings from the clothesline attached between the shed and a tree. The line's rusty pulley squeaks as towels and swimsuits and T-shirts swing in the light breeze. Aidan looks over at the car where Shayne sits, reading a book. He wonders what it'd be like to live in a car.

When he hears someone shout, "Hole in one!" his attention is drawn to two of his cousins, Scottie and James, playing golf. For two more holes Aidan watches. As James tees off on the fifth hole, Aidan wonders what's taking Connor so long.

"Do we need two buckets?" Aidan asks, trying to be helpful. "We could share this one?"

Connor thrusts his head out the door, his expression clearly conveying who the most useless brother on the planet is. "Yes, we need two buckets. Otherwise, the frog hops away."

"Oh. Right."

"There's another bucket somewhere. I saw Doctor washing the mud from his car a couple of days ago, with two buckets." Connor points at the gravel road that splits the property.

"What colour was it?" Aidan asks.

"Huh?"

"The other bucket."

Connor stands in the shed door. "This one is yellow, that means the other one was . . . uh . . . maybe . . . red?"

"Don't ask me. I didn't see the Doctor washing his car."

"Well, he was." Connor stands there, on the step above Aidan, thinking.

"Want me to look?" Aidan asks, craning his neck around Connor to peek into the dark confines of the shed.

Connor pauses, then jumps down onto the grass. "Sure."

"Really?"

"Why not?"

"Really really?"

"Hurry up." Connor waves Aidan into the shed.

Aidan pokes his head in. It's a tight space with hooks and hangers on the walls and boxes on the floor. Shelves filled with grown-up stuff rise the height of the back wall: extension cords, tarps, the grill on which an uncle cooked the deer sausages made from his car accident in the Yukon, drill bits, rubber boots, an indoor/outdoor vacuum needed for the next time the toilet backs up, empty jam jars, tubes of caulk, a big red toolbox, cans of old paint, and overfull baskets resting on the top shelf. A wooden stepladder hangs on a side wall. Between two of the ladder's steps is a spider's web. He can't tell if a spider still lives there or if it's just a cobweb. Under the ladder sits a big cardboard box that could contain a bucket. Aidan steps inside for a look.

The shed goes black. Hockey puck black. Aidan doesn't move for fear of knocking against the shelves, or the mower, or the spider web. He thinks about the spider. Then he thinks about the spider in the dark shed. Then he thinks about himself and the spider in the dark shed. He isn't sure whether there's a spider or not, but it seems a much bigger problem in the dark than when he was only peering in. Panic swirls through his chest.

"Let me out!"

Connor doesn't answer. Aidan feels stupid, falling for Connor's prank. But he also wants out. He touches what he hopes is the door. It is. Aidan pushes against the door. It doesn't move. Aidan's cheeks tighten, and his eyes start to water. It feels like he's been in here a long time. Too long. He shoulders the door with all fifty-eight of his pounds. It doesn't move. Panic shoots through his body as the thought of being trapped in the dark shed shoves any other thought out of his head. He takes a step back and ploughs into the door as hard as he can.

The door flies open, and Aidan tumbles onto the grass. The sunlight is blinding. By the time Aidan stands and brushes himself off, Connor is halfway down the path to the back door of the cottage with the yellow bucket in his hand.

Wiping his left eye, Aidan considers abandoning Connor and the whole frog expedition. He could golf with Scottie and James. Or he could go swimming. Or he could go tell his mom what happened. But he isn't hurt. He can play golf anytime. He already went swimming today. And he's never caught a frog before.

Aidan sprints after Connor and hollers, "Wait for me!"

They search the cottage for a second bucket. They can't find the Doctor. They ask everyone else, but no one knows where, or even if there is one.

"Let's go ask Mac," Connor says.

"Mac?"

"The guy that lives right next door. He came to the barbeque?"

"Oh, him."

The boys duck through the large birch trees that separate the Camp from Mac's property. Mac, in a white T-shirt and pale blue shorts, sits in a chair on the porch, reading a newspaper.

As they approach, the newspaper folds down and Mac asks, "Can I help you?"

"Hey, Mac," Connor asks, "do you have a bucket?"

Mac asks, "It's Connor and . . .?"

"Aidan," Aidan says.

Mac points to Connor's hand. "You already have a bucket."

Connor looks down at his hand, then up again. "We need two."

"Going to the frog pond?" Mac looks up at the sky. "A good day for it. I think there's a bucket in the attic." Mac folds his paper under his arm and stands. "Do you two want some juice while I look?"

Sitting in a chair on Mac's porch, Aidan scrapes the last drop of juice from the side of his glass with the tip of his tongue. "What's the deal with Mac?"

"He's an American."

"What does he do?"

"What do you mean 'What does he do?' He lives in America." Connor shakes his head.

Aidan isn't sure he got an answer to his question, but given Connor's reaction, decides it isn't worth pursuing. He gets up, walks to the edge of the grass, gathers a handful of stones and piles all but one of them at the end of Mac's dock. The stone in his hand he throws as far as he can. It hits the water with a satisfying plop and sinks.

"Skip it!" Connor calls from Mac's porch.

"I don't know how."

"I'll show you." Connor pops up from his chair and jogs out to Aidan. He picks up a stone and, side-armed, flings it across the surface of the water where it hits and bounces and hits and bounces and hits and bounces again. "Like that!"

Aidan takes a stone, rears back, then flings it with all his might. Plop.

Aidan notices a loon out in the middle of the lake. The loon seems unimpressed.

"No, like this." Connor moves his arm back and forth, side-armed, flicking his wrist. Then he lets the stone go. It skips along the surface again.

Aidan practises the motion, then throws a stone out as hard as he can.

Plop. The loon dives under the surface of the lake.

Connor laughs. "You gotta make it go along the surface of the water. Flat-like. Throw it kind of like a frisbee, only backwards."

Which instruction is a whole lot of good to Aidan, who, as Connor knows, hasn't mastered the art of throwing a frisbee. Aidan tries. Connor demonstrates. Until, starting not to care anymore, Aidan lets one go.

Skip. Skip. Plop. The loon trills from the water on Aidan's left.

"Yes!" Connor shouts and hugs Aidan. Then, remembering himself, he lets go and says, "Not bad. Now see if you can get more than two skips."

They continue skipping stones until, as Aidan grabs a smooth, flat stone, with a white stripe cut diagonally across its black surface, Mac comes out holding a blue bucket. "Here you go, boys!"

Connor dashes to the porch. Aidan shoves the stone in his pocket and follows. He can show Connor later.

Aidan carries the yellow bucket and practises whistling. He whistles that song about the guy in the store who's lost his glasses and can't see. Connor carries Mac's blue bucket. He doesn't whistle. The buckets swing back and forth on their handles as the boys walk. Aidan varies his cadence to see if his bucket will keep time. Every time he changes his cadence, the swing changes. He tries going slower, and the bucket swings slower. He goes faster and the bucket swings—

"Oof!"

"Would you watch where you're going?" Connor shouts.

"Uh, sorry, I was trying to see if—"

"I don't care what you were doing, watch where you're going." Connor stomps down the path through the trees.

When they come out of the trees onto the beach, Aidan squats by the water's edge to see if there are any big fish. The water is shallower here than at the cottage. He can see more: the sandy bottom, clams embedded in the sand, minnows darting around, but no big fish. He never sees big fish at the beach. Maybe big fish don't like beaches.

Where the sand turns to grass, the boys turn inland, cutting between cottages to a dirt lane, still muddy from the night's rain. Aidan jumps as hard as he can into the middle of the biggest puddle in the lane, soaking himself.

"What's the big idea?" Connor cries as he uses the crook of his arm to wipe his face.

"Jeez, sorry, I didn't mean . . ."

Connor punches him in the arm and turns away, fuming. Aidan rubs his arm, shuffles after him, then stays three or four steps behind his brother, avoiding all puddles.

They come to a T-intersection with a gravel road. Connor leads them across onto a footpath bordered by long grass that cuts through some trees. The path narrows and Aidan's bucket brushes the stalks of grass as he passes. At the end, the boys emerge onto a small, mossy landing.

Reeds and cattails higher than Aidan's head grow in clumps across the surface of a pond. Blackish-green water spreads, shallow and murky and dark. Leaves and scum and lily pads float on the surface. The air is fragrant with decay.

"Yuck!" Aidan says, "This is a swamp!"

"Shhh!"

"But look at it!" Aidan sweeps his arms in front of himself.

"Shhh!" Connor shushes again.

"Why should I?"

"For chrissake Aidan! Would you be quiet?" Connor hisses, "Every frog in the pond is gonna know we're here!" Connor squats at the water's edge. Aidan leans against a tree, as quietly as he can, watching his brother scan the water. Connor doesn't stop the sweep of his gaze for the cattails, or the duck that paddles by, or the water strider on the surface. Aidan can see him searching for some sign of, Aidan presumes, a frog. Birds dart from one tree to another, unconcerned with the two boys below.

Finally, unable to contain himself any longer, Aidan whispers, "What'cha doing?"

"Looking for their eyes. That's all you can see when they're in the water."

"What do they look like?"

Connor scowls at Aidan. "Like frog eyes, ya moron. What do you think?"

Aidan tries to look for frog eyes without knowing what he is looking for. After a few fruitless minutes, he decides it's better to wait for Connor. He pulls the stone out of his pocket and traces the white line down the middle with his thumb. He's tempted to try to skip it on the pond, but that would likely be a bad idea. A squirrel natters in the trees behind him. A frog galumphs somewhere. A mosquito whines by his ear. He hears a breath of wind through the reeds and the chirrup of a cricket or grasshopper. There are other sounds he can't identify. He moves closer to his brother, who is still watching the pond.

"There!" Connor whispers, pointing to his left.

"Where?" Aidan half whispers back.

"Right there," Connor pokes his finger in the same direction and looks to see if Aidan is watching. "The two little bumps on the surface of the water, right by the water lily."

Aidan peers along the water surface following Connor's finger. He sees insects looping an inch or two above the water, islets of pond scum, the water lily Connor mentioned, and a large clump of reeds into which a water strider vanishes. Then he sees them: two small bumps at the surface of the water, almost the same colour as the water, but a shade lighter. When one of the bumps twitches, Aidan forgets Connor's warnings.

"I see him!" He springs up.

But before he is upright, Connor grabs his shirt and tugs him down. "Quiet." He backs away, motioning for Aidan to follow. Back at the tree trunk, Connor says, "Okay, now do you want to catch a frog?"

Aidan nods.

"Then listen carefully and do what I say."

Aidan nods again.

"You take your bucket, and I take mine. You go off to the left. I go off to the right. Watch the frog's eyes . . ."

Aidan is excited and hears only half of what Connor says, but the idea is to go slow and basically do whatever Connor does.

When Connor creeps to the right, Aidan follows. Connor motions for Aidan to go to the left. Aidan goes left. He watches Connor creep to the edge of the pond, holding his bucket high. Aidan does the same. At the edge of the water, Connor nods; this is a bit confusing as Aidan doesn't remember being told what to do for a nod. He nods back. This satisfies Connor. Aidan tries to be as quiet as he can, but with blood pounding in his eardrums and the forest sounds and the fact that he is about to step into the water, Aidan can't be sure the frog isn't aware of their presence already.

Connor enters the water, making few ripples and less noise. Aidan follows his lead. The frog doesn't move. Connor takes a second careful step. Aidan does likewise. The frog doesn't move. Connor takes a third step, stops, and raises his hand. Aidan starts to take a third step. Connor gestures excitedly. Aidan stops, balancing on one foot. The frog's eyes are moving, but it doesn't jump. Aidan raises his eyebrows at Connor, hoping Connor understands that he can barely maintain his balance. Connor holds up his hand. Aidan feels his grounded foot tilt slightly. Connor looks in the direction of the frog. The bucket in Aidan's hand wavers with his balance. Connor pats the air with his arm. Aidan feels his hips start to tilt with his foot. Then tilt further. Finally, Connor motions downwards with his hand. Aidan lowers his foot into the water only slightly more awkwardly than he intended. The frog doesn't move.

Aidan is close enough now to see the frog's spots, its shiny skin, webbed fingers, and hind legs splayed limply beneath the surface of the water. If the frog knows the boys are there, it isn't letting on. Connor points to Aidan's bucket, then at the back of the frog. As slowly as he can, Aidan places his bucket behind the frog. The frog doesn't move.

Swiftly, Connor brings his bucket down in front of the frog. Aidan closes his eyes, turns his head away, expecting a thump or bang or something in his bucket. He hears a splash, then another. And then another.

"Damn!" Connor swears.

Aidan opens his eyes and asks, "What happened?"

"He got away. He jumped sideways before I could get my bucket to yours. I think he knew you were behind him."

They go back to shore. Connor sits cross-legged on the moss with his elbows on his knees, his chin resting on folded hands. His eyes are closed. Aidan sits down beside Connor and rubs the stone in his pocket. Two dragonflies, stuck together, dart over the water and around the clumps of tall grass. Uncle Ed told Aidan that when they fly together like that, the dragonflies are mating, but Ed didn't explain what mating meant. To Aidan, dragonflies look like aliens. They eat mosquitoes. They are colourful and fast, and they don't bite.

"Okay," Connor says quietly. "We try again. But to make sure the frog doesn't hop out the side, I'm going to bring my bucket down, right into yours. We'll be trapping him with nowhere to go." Connor looks at Aidan, waiting for confirmation of his genius.

The first thing that comes to Aidan's mind with this new plan is a frog leg or arm getting caught between the buckets' lips. That would hurt the frog. Aidan doesn't want to hurt a frog. He raises the issue with Connor.

"Then how else are we going to make sure the frog doesn't hop away?" Connor asks, hands on hips.

After some thought, Aidan offers, "What if we blocked the sides with our legs?"

"What?" Connor asks, annoyance ringing off the trees.

"At the side of the frog when the buckets come together. Like, if I first place the back bucket—like before—so he doesn't know it's there. Then, you bring your bucket down and, at the same time, we both move to the side."

Connor says nothing for a while. Then he shrugs and says, "That's stupid. It'll never work."

Aidan feels his cheeks warm.

Then Connor says, "Oh, what the heck. We might as well give it a try."

On the walk back, Aidan gets to carry the bucket with the frog some of the time. Along the muddy lane, both boys jump in puddles, laughing as they soak each other. At the beach, they stop to look for big fish and use a stick to try to open a clam. On the path through the trees, they whistle the theme song from *The Andy Griffith Show*, both off pitch. As they come up the path to Mac's house, Aidan's thumb rubs the smooth surface of the stone in his pocket. He sees Scottie, sitting on the end of the yellow dock, wrapped in a towel, smiling at his mom.

They knock on Mac's door. After a few moments, Mac comes from the kitchen and waves at them.

"Well, boys," Mac answers, coming out through the screen door with a stack of folded bed sheets. "How'd it go?"

Aidan passes Mac the yellow bucket.

Mac peers in. "He's a big one! How'd you catch him?"

Connor explains, "The first one got away. He jumped sideways. But the second time we covered the sides with our legs, and he had nowhere to go. He jumped backward into the bucket."

Mac looks impressed. "Using your legs to cut him off, eh? Good idea. Who thought of that?"

Aidan takes a small step forward.

Connor answers, "I did. Aidan's never even been frog hunting before."

Aidan's hand curls around the stone in his pocket.

SHAYNE: OWLS

It gets warm in the car. I roll up my sleeping bag and put my
pillow on top of the roll. A family of woodpeckers taps on a dead
spruce tree trunk in the middle of the row between the Camp
and the neighbouring yard. The birds are black and white with
stripes on their wings and dots on their breast. One of them—I
think it's the dad—has a tuft of red on the top of his head. As the
woodpeckers flit around the rotten tree, there's some movement
from the neighbour's green and grey cottage. An older guy comes
out the back door carrying a garbage bag. He's stocky and balding,
in shorts, a T-shirt, and a Red Sox cap. He moves slowly. He might
even have a limp, but I can't tell for sure. Through the gaps in the
row of spruce trees I see him go into a shed, then I lose sight of him.

Dad used to pull a book down from the shelf of our den to show
me what kind of bird we'd seen riding our bikes or hiking in the
river valley. He got a big kick out of sitting on our porch with his
binoculars, calling out as many different birds as he could. One
time, he found an owl's nest in a tree by the bridge spanning the
river near our house. He was excited enough that when I got home
from school, he already had a pack and a lantern ready. We made
peanut butter sandwiches, left Mom a note, and climbed down the
ravine to the riverbank across from the nest. We sat on a tarp at
the river's edge as the light changed from dusk into night: taking
in the muskrats swimming through the bullrushes, a heron's
stillness then sudden strike of beak through the water surface, the
clover-scented banks. We sat all night watching the river, the owl,
and her babies.

I fell asleep with my head in his lap, but he stayed awake the whole night, watching those owls watching over me. When dawn broke, he shook me awake. We climbed up out of the ravine and stumbled home. He helped me into bed, pulled down the blinds, and closed the door of my room.

I heard them downstairs as I pulled the covers up over my head.

"He's got school today," Mom said.

"He's got school every day."

"Yeah, like every other kid." Mom's voice got a little louder. "He isn't doing that well, you know. He needs to be in school; needs to focus. I don't want him to fall behind."

"He said he's trying. That's all we can ask him to do. These things take time." Then Dad talked slower, like he always did when he needed you to listen. "School's important, but this is an owl's nest. There were owlets. Something he might never see again, and he'll always remember."

Mom said something I couldn't hear.

Then Dad said, "I'll call the school. He can still do the work he'll miss. We can do it together this afternoon."

"Fine. I, at least, have to go to work now." I heard some banging and some rattling around in the kitchen before her voice again, "In the future can we at least talk about these things *before* you do them?"

The old guy comes back out of the shed with no garbage bag. He stops and watches the woodpeckers, pulls the Red Sox cap off, wipes his brow, and replaces it. He looks up at the tapping bird and grins, then he looks through the trees right at me, tips the bill of his cap and with a nod, goes back into his cottage.

I am left alone with the woodpeckers, the tree, and the memory of those owls. I can't remember what we were doing in school that week, but I can remember the wet, earthy smell of the riverbank, the sound of fish jumping out of the river at the moon, and the eyes of that owl.

I remember Dad, too.

MAC

Mac brushes his teeth, trying not to focus on the greyish-purple crescents under his eyes. He slaps cold water on his face and wet-combs his thin grey-brown hair. With a yawn, he puts on a white undershirt, blue shorts, a pair of white calf-length socks, and loafers. He shuffles downstairs, stoops to turn on the little gas heater by the back door, then turns into the kitchen.

The Mr. Coffee isn't finished brewing. Mac pulls a can of concentrate from the freezer and plops the contents into a pitcher. He mashes the frozen cylinder into shards, adds water, and stirs, then pours himself a highball of juice. He can't escape the tug of pancakes with bacon. Humming and sipping his juice, Mac mixes the batter and greases a pan. He flips six golden-brown fluffy pancakes onto a small platter and places them in the centre of the kitchen table. While the bacon fries, he finds a bottle of maple syrup in the pantry and adds a dusting of icing sugar for garnish.

He sits at the kitchen table, fork and knife in hand, but his enthusiasm fades as he looks around the empty cottage and out the screen door to the lake. He only manages to eat two pancakes and a single strip of bacon before abandoning the meal, leaving his dishes and the extra food on the counter to be put away later. He pours himself a coffee, presses a newspaper under his arm, and leaves the kitchen.

As he backs out through the screen door, flecks of grey float down around him. He scans the cottage face. Grey and mint-green paint peels off the side of the cottage in strips the width of playing cards. Easing himself into a chair on the porch, Mac places the newspaper on one chair arm, his coffee on the other, and puts on the ballcap he keeps under the chair for the sun. He gazes out across Grand Lake, down to the beach on his left, and over to the cottage on his right.

Over the last few days, the Murphy clan has congregated at the lake. Their cottage always was the centre of activity, but with the arrival of a third generation, the place has become dizzyingly entropic. Yesterday afternoon, he watched from this same chair as the older grandkids leapt off the dock with their best tricks, encouraged by adult chants and yells. The chanting parents were children doing the same jumps into the lake twenty-five years ago.

He unfolds the paper and removes the sports section before dropping the remainder on the grass. Jack Nicklaus has won another US Open, the Reds already look like a lock for the pennant, and the Olympics in Munich are only weeks away. He pulls out a pencil and works on the crossword as a breeze from Blueberry Point ruffles the corner of the page. After getting as far as he can with the crossword, Mac is surveying the arts section when he hears something—or rather someone—on the other side of the page.

"Can I help you?" he asks, folding down the paper.

"Hey, Mac! Do you have a bucket?"

Two boys stand at the bottom of the porch steps. Clearly brothers, they are six inches apart in height, but share sharp chins, high cheekbones, sun-chapped lips, and deep tans. The smaller boy, his right shin sporting a grass-stained bandage, wears cut-off jean shorts, a T-shirt, rubber boots, and a ball cap. The taller one also wears jean shorts and rubber boots, but sports a black mesh football jersey with some Canadian football team logo Mac doesn't recognize.

In his mind, Mac rolls through the names of the kids staying at the Murphy place. "It's Connor and . . .?"

"Aidan," the smaller one says.

Mac points to Connor's hand. "You already have a bucket."

Connor looks down at the bucket in his hand, then looks up. "We need two."

"Going to the frog pond?"

The boys nod.

Mac looks up into a blue sky, noting one small cloud. "A good day for it."

The two boys look at him, say nothing.

"I think there's a bucket in the attic." Mac gets up from his chair. "Do you two want some juice while I look?"

After bringing the boys their juice, Mac steps through the front sunroom that Lily insisted on decorating with anchors, starfish, and ships' steering wheels—even after he pointed out that the cottage was on a lake. In the kitchen, the memory of hearing Lily's scream as he fished on the dock overtakes him. He had dropped his fishing rod into the lake, charged up the lawn, and burst through the screen door only to find Kyle and Toby heatedly explaining to her, in this very spot, why the breadbox *was* a perfect place to house their frog. All three directed their upset to him when he collapsed onto the sofa laughing.

Heading upstairs, Mac passes a framed family photo on the wall. In it, Lily and the boys smile and look at the camera, a time when she was still here. Mac was always scared for them, proud of them, or infuriated by their independent streak.

At the second floor, he stops to catch his breath beside an oak chest hand built by his grandfather. Lily hated the chest because it was large, always in the way, the wrong colour. To Mac it was a consecrated vessel, made for them by the man who took him in when, after his parents' divorce, his father dissolved into drink and his mother shuttled from apartment to motel room to rooming house, following the next man she knew would finally be the right one. His grandfather, seeing the seven-year-old boy bounced from one parent to the other and back again across the state, took custody and provided the security and discipline of farm life. In the fall, after each harvest, his grandfather would pull Mac into the woodworking shop at the back of the barn where Mac learned, as much as anything about woodwork, the capacity for quiet and love that he drew on when Lily entered his life.

Turning from the chest, he passes two paintings on the hallway wall. The first, a paint-by-numbers sea otter Kyle finished when he was ten. The other, Lily in the lake, painted by Doc Murphy, a gift to Mac the year after her sickness. Lily's eyes out-blue the water she treads. The floral shower cap she insisted on wearing to swim, her expression the pleasant perseverance of a reluctant lake bather who needs to wash but hates to be cold. To Mac, it is only yesterday she would stand and shiver in a towel on the porch.

Yesterday and a lifetime ago.

In the first months after she was gone, Mac received invitations to dinners and parties with the friends they had shared. When at last he plucked up the courage to accept one, he arrived too early. His hosts, people with whom he and Lily had spent many days, were politely uncomfortable as they discussed her, his now being alone, and what he was up to. Both sides of the coffee table waited anxiously for the arrival of more guests. When others finally did come, Mac couldn't escape talk of Lily and sympathetic suggestions for his participation in activities, each new conversation an exercise in self-immolation.

He staggered home, sweating, shaky, crushed by her absence.

The next day, he dug through her writing desk for a thank-you card and dropped it in the hosts' mailbox, lacking the strength to ring their doorbell. Over the next days and weeks, he was careful to let people know how busy he was and what trip he had planned for the weekend now that he was free to do what he wanted. In this way, he scarred and healed and numbed himself to her absence.

Mac pulls on a short piece of rope hanging from the ceiling at the end of the second-floor hallway. A wooden ladder drops to his feet. He tests it with a shake before hauling himself up, trying to remember the last time he climbed to the top of the cottage.

The attic, smaller and more cluttered than he remembers, has exposed beams, a peaked ceiling, and unfinished window frames. Boxes, chests, and old furniture cram the space. He lifts a quilt, releasing a cloud of dust, turns, and sneezes loudly, causing more dust to fly up from a plastic milk crate full of LPs. Thelonious,

Chet, Miles, Charlie, the sound of his weekend trolls through clubs in Harlem with the gang from Rugby Road. It was all "noise" to her, while the milky universe of Perry Como and Andy Williams that she brought with her from Belle Haven usually sent him in search of that lightbulb that needed changing.

In a blue and brass metal chest, he finds old board games: Risk, Monopoly, Stratego, and Battleship. Games they would play after sundown, around the dining room table, sharing a bowl of popcorn. The boys fighting over who got to go first; Lily reading and enforcing the rules. Whoever won—he made sure it was never him—had bragging rights until the next day.

He discovers four unlabelled cardboard boxes filled with stuffies, Lego, old towels, and older clothes. She threw nothing out, not even the tatty old pillow loved by her long-dead tomcat, Felix. Folded neatly at the top of one box are the red trunks Toby wore on his swim to Blueberry Point. When Toby began to tire in the last few hundred yards, Lily, in the boat they rowed to support him, pleaded for Mac to pull him out. Mac refused, watching Toby closely. For the rest of that summer, guests had to smile politely and listen, again, to her proud, crimson-cheeked account of how Toby swam to the Point, failing to mention her own attempts to abort the event.

Mac sits down in her old rocking chair. He recalls the sound of her wheezes as she rocked, the two of them reading into the night while the boys slept. Her snort when the story was racy or ridiculous. The smell of chamomile tea steaming on the table beside her. His annoyance with her need to read random sentences aloud to him, especially, it seemed, when he was engrossed in his own book. The puff of breath from the corner of her mouth to move her bangs and better see the page. The cashmere sweaters she wore, one over her shoulders, another over her legs.

Lily.

The first summer after, Mac and the boys went to the lake as always. They packed the same fishing gear and swim trunks, loaded the car with the same food, stopped at the same burger place on the trip up. But when they arrived, she filled every crevice. On the third night, as he was turning in, he found Kyle sitting by himself at the kitchen table.

"Hey, what'cha doing?" Mac asked.

Without turning, Kyle said, "I don't know. It feels nice."

"What does?"

"I can sort of feel her here. You even kept her chair out." Kyle pointed to the embroidered cushion on one of the chairs under the table.

The ground tilted beneath Mac's feet.

"Remember how she would spend days drying and salting the trout we caught, like her grandmother had taught her to do? And then on cold nights here, she would bring out warm milk and the salted fish with mayonnaise on crackers. We'd sit around this table pretending it was delicious so as not to hurt her feelings?"

Mac sat at the table, his cheeks warming. "Toby would insist on hot chocolate."

"I'd forgotten that."

They sat at the table together, not speaking. Kyle placed his hand on Mac's forearm, his jaw clenching, and his lower lip trembling until he could say, "I guess I keep hoping that if I sit here, long enough, quietly enough, maybe she'll come by with a mug of milk and some of that dreadful fish."

Kyle's nose dripped onto the table, and he wiped the surface with the back of his hand. The chair scraped as he pushed away and went upstairs, leaving Mac alone at the table with three empty chairs. At that moment, Mac knew their return to the lake was too soon, her absence too raw.

The next few summers the boys had jobs and girlfriends, Europe to explore, or classes to attend. Mac couldn't face the prospect of her ghost on his own, instead chose to stay in the city to practise his golf game, making no real progress. For a few years, he rented the cottage, avoiding the place and its memories as best he could.

But this year when the agent called, Mac, surprising himself, decided not to list.

Alone, he packed up, got in the car, drove up the I-95 into Canada. In the dark, he turned onto the dirt road to the lake. He unpacked to the familiar sound of water lapping against the retaining wall, placed his canvas rod case in the corner of the muck room and hung his clothes neatly in the bedroom closet. He found a can of spaghetti and a can of brown beans and warmed them up together in a pot for dinner. Sipping coffee on the porch, he watched moths bump stupidly, again and again, against the one outside electric bulb that still worked. He crawled into bed to the mournful sound of a loon. He was back.

Mac puttered around the place in the mornings, replacing light bulbs, oiling locks, removing storm windows, and beating dust from rugs. He fished from the dock in the afternoon. He watched the sunset in the evening. He sipped coffee on the porch at night with the moths. He followed that loon around the lake with his binoculars, and, when he glimpsed a chick on her back, a dormant part of his soul shook itself awake.

A week after Mac arrived, Doc Murphy knocked on the screen door and invited him to dinner. "It'll be something grilled, buns, and maybe a salad. Come if you want to. Whenever you want. Stay however long you like. Don't bring a thing. There's plenty. The grandkids are putting on a show during dessert. You know, singing, unrehearsed dance routines, and baton twirling."

"Thanks," Mac answered.

The Doctor chuckled and shook his head, "Don't thank me yet, you haven't heard the singing." He waved over his shoulder, humming to himself as he nimbly stepped off the porch, across the lawn, and along the retaining wall back to his own cottage.

Mac felt anxious the rest of the day, thinking about the invitation. He wondered what he should wear, what to bring. He took different bottles off the wine rack and examined them, considering which one might go with burgers. He washed a shirt and hung it with thoughts of a pressing. In the end, he remembered the Doctor's words and where he was. He left the wine bottles on their rack and his shirt hanging on the door. He slipped out the back door then stood on the top step, listening through the row of spruce trees that separated his property from their back lawn. He heard a cackle of laughter and a concerned voice ask, "Who in their right mind hosts a Tupperware party with a house full of sick kids, paint fumes, and a new baby?"

He squeezed through the spruce and, for a few moments, stood alone surveying the commotion on the Murphys' back lawn, questioning his decision to come. Then Betsy waved to him, patted the chair beside her, and continued the conversation she was having with a child wearing a unicorn floatie around her waist.

"But Grammy, why would a leprechaun make candy all the way up in the forest?"

"You can't expect them to make candy in the lake," Betsy said sternly. "Leprechauns can't swim."

The cacophony on the lawn continued, unperturbed by his presence. As he navigated legs and hands and towels and groups of chairs, he dissolved into the crowd.

When Mac finally dropped into the chair beside Betsy, there was a shout from the grill, "Mac! Red hot or burger?"

A robin chastises him from the attic window, a leaf in its beak. Mac sits in the dusty silence a moment longer, then slaps his thighs. He stands, stiff, and hobbles over to a mop leaning aslant the roof wall. Beside the mop, partially draped by a torn curtain, he finds the bucket. He takes it, walks over to the hole in the floor where the ladder descends, and drops it through with a clunk. He uses both hands to support his weight down to the second-floor hallway and taps the family photo as he descends to the first floor carrying the bucket. Back in the kitchen, he notes the dirty breakfast dishes and uneaten food.

"Here you go, boys," he says, as he pushes out through the screen door. He holds the bucket high.

The boys run from the dock, where they were skipping stones.

"Thanks for the drink," Connor says, as he trots up to Mac.

"Yeah, it was great!" Aidan chimes in.

"Have fun," Mac says. "Let me know how you do. It'd be good to know whether frogs are any smarter these days."

The brothers disappear down the same beach path Mac and his boys travelled to get to the same frog pond.

He gathers up the juice glasses and places them in the kitchen sink with the breakfast dishes. He turns the water on full hot, adds some dish soap, and watches the sink erupt with lemony suds. When the sink is full, he plunges his hands into the all-but-scalding water and bites his lip as he washes each piece. The dishes he leaves to dry in the mid-morning air and puts away the leftovers. Opening the garbage bin, he touches something moist and sticky and almost pulls away: pancakes stuck to the outside of the pail. He flips them from the lid into the liner bag and then licks syrup from his thumb. He gathers the bag's mouth into two strands and ties them closed. Standing slowly, nursing his stiff knees, Mac carries the bag out to the shed and lifts the lid off a large bin. As he drops the smaller bag, fruit flies swarm up into his face followed by the odour of rotting banana peels and the fish stew he had for supper.

Back in the kitchen, he finds a dry dish towel, wipes down the counter, then the table, and cleans away a squashed fruit fly clinging to the window over the sink. Stepping back, Mac surveys the kitchen and feels she would approve. From a cupboard above the stove, he pulls down a bottle of Balvenie and pours two fingers of whisky into a glass tumbler. Carrying the tumbler, he sits at the kitchen table and plays with the fringe of her seat cushion on the chair beside him. He checks the hanging kitchen light for dead bugs, then looks over at the avocado-green telephone attached to the wall by the fridge, fingers a knot of wood on the table, and slings back the contents of the tumbler.

His chair scrapes the floor as he rises. He picks up the receiver and dials. After a few seconds, the line rings through.

"Hello?" a familiar voice on the other end answers.

"Hey, Toby. It's Dad. What're you doing this weekend?"

SHAYNE: THE FROG

I need to pee again, so I get out of the car. I'm over by the shed when I hear voices on the grass near the cottage. Two kids and the Doctor stand around a yellow bucket sitting on the grass.

"It's a big one," the Doctor says.

"He keeps trying to get out," the littler kid says. He's the same kid who fell out of the shed earlier. "We don't have a lid."

The three of them lean over and peer into the bucket.

"He needs to stay wet, Connor. I'm not sure there's enough water in there," the Doctor says.

Connor must be the tall one. He turns to the little kid and says, "Aidan, go get some more water from the lake."

"Get it yourself," the little kid—Aidan I guess—says, scowling at Connor. "Mac told us the frog needs more water. You didn't listen."

"I'll go get him some water," the Doctor straightens up. "Because that's important." He walks off toward the cottage.

I want to see the frog and wander over to the bucket.

"You've caught a green frog," I say.

"It's a bullfrog," Aidan says.

"No. It's a green frog." I point to his head. "You can tell by the size of its ear. A bullfrog's ear is bigger than its eyes."

Connor looks at me. "How'd ya know that?"

"My dad taught me."

"Our dad made us take the frog back outside when we tried to bring him in the living room," Aidan says.

"Can I pick him up?" I ask.

"You can," Connor says, "but he might pee on you."

"Yeah, I know, but as long as my hands are wet, it won't hurt him."

"Your hands?" Aidan asks.

"You have to wet your hands before you touch him; that way you don't make him sick."

He nods like he knew this all along.

I splash some canteen water on my hands and pick up the frog. I hold him tight. He's a good size. I can feel his heart pounding. There's a cool trickle on my hand.

"He peed!" Aidan points at my hand laughing.

The frog's eyes dart left then right then left again. While I like holding him and think he's great, I feel for the frog. He and I could share impressions if I talked frog: neither of us are in the place we want to be, we were both minding our own business when the world changed, and we don't like other people watching us when all we want to be is left alone. I put the frog back in the bucket.

"Thanks," I say rinsing my hands again and wiping them on my shorts. Having seen the frog, I feel exposed. My curiosity might've got the better of me for a moment, but I head back to the car as the Doctor returns from the cottage carrying a jug of water.

As soon I've got the door locked, I dig out my notebook and draw a picture of the frog. My green pencil is dull, and I don't have a sharpener. I can't get him all coloured in, but at least I get a sketch. I'll have a record. You can always finish the sketch later. Dad did that a lot when we were out hiking—start a sketch in the field and finish it later in his office. It's a good way to make sure that what you want to remember is as accurate as possible. All his sketches are still in a folder on his desk. When we get back home maybe I'll go and look through them. Or maybe I won't. Someday I should.

The cottage door bangs open. A girl, holding a doll, skips across the grass to the bucket. She looks in, jumps back, then runs up toward the forest. I lose sight of her as she passes behind the far side of the cabin. No one runs after her. I can see the Doctor watching her, and he doesn't move, so it must be okay. I go back to drawing.

As I finish my sketch of the frog, I look over at the bucket where he is.

The frog in the bucket; me in the car.
It's hard to say who's more trapped.

AN L

Daddy said my lips were turning blue, to go inside and warm up. Everyone else got to stay swimming. The first thing I did when I got inside was go into the bathroom and look at my lips. They weren't blue. Daddy was fibbing.

I went upstairs to look for Wendy. I had to go past Fiona's bed and Anne's bed and Connor's bed and Aidan's bed and the bed shared by Dylan and Liam before I got to mine. Wendy was still sleeping. Lazy bones. I scooped her up then looked under the bed. It wasn't there. I walked over to the old dresser against the wall with the chipped white paint. I started opening drawers, but they were full of clothes and quilts and other people's stuff. Way down in the bottom drawer I saw my backpack. I yanked it out, slung it over my shoulder, then hopped back downstairs with Wendy under my arm.

The living room was empty. I looked at the felt triangles stuck high on the walls. My favourite flag is one that Mommy told me said "San Francisco," which is a famous city with a big bridge. The flag shows a man and a woman jumping onto a trolley car and a man in a hat smiling at them. The man and woman together is what you call 'in love.'

Out the big windows on the far side of the living room, I could see the two large pinecone trees at the side of the cottage. Yesternight, the wind banged the trees against the side of the cottage. I was lying in bed, but I got scared and couldn't sleep. I snuck downstairs and crawled into bed with Mommy. Daddy wasn't there. Mommy said there wasn't room for him. There was room for me. She let me stay the whole night.

I took Wendy over to the giant gas heater under the big windows. The heater was roaring there at the end of the living room. I'm not scared of the heater anymore. Wendy needed a hug, though. We sat down against the big, white couch that Daddy sleeps on when he's watching the baseball game on TV. The couch has buckles on it that you can't undo—I've tried. I took a blanket from the couch.

We spread the blanket on the carpet. I balled up my towel for Wendy to sit against and not fall over. She doesn't mind wet, except for the time I dropped her in my tub. She had to hang upside down on the clothesline for two days. She didn't like that. We pulled the stuff out of the backpack: a teapot, teacups, plates, two forks, a spoon, and the food—it's pretend. Wendy set two places while I made the tea. Red Rose, like Daddy drinks. Lots of sugar.

Then my auntie Candi, whose real name is Candace and who hugs too hard and kisses too much, limped into the room with a mug. Scottie said she had a surgery on her leg. I couldn't see the surgery, but her knee is wide and droopy. She dropped into the big chair by the bathroom door and took a sip from her mug. I pretended I was busy, but adults never leave you alone when they think they have something important to talk about.

"Does your doll have a name, dear?" she asked me.

"Wendy," I said without turning to look at her. I was trying to make the tea.

Candi didn't notice. "Does Wendy have a boyfriend?"

"Yes." Mommy says it's not polite to ignore people, even when you want to.

"She does! What's his name?"

I poured tea for Wendy and me and answered, "Buttercup."

"Buttercup?" Candi scrunched up her voice. "That sounds like a horse's name."

"It is."

"How can a horse be her boyfriend?"

"Buttercup's a *boy* horse."

Mommy came into the room holding a coffee mug in her hand. A cigarette was pressed between her lips. Then aunt Tommie followed her, carrying a mug in one hand and a plate in the other. Both still had their pajamas on and tight curlers in their hair. They smelled like the hairdresser's shop. Mommy sometimes makes me come along if Daddy doesn't come home the night before she has an appointment. The hairdresser is okay, because she lets me play with the bobby pins and curlers, and if you do it right you can make a long snake out of them. But it still smells funny there.

Mommy and Tommie sat in the armchairs against the stairs to the loft. With all the adults here, I wanted to go somewhere new, but we'd already poured our tea. Wendy wondered if her friend Holly was having tea too.

". . . and get this: he asked Fred," Tommie said.

"Fred!" Mommy asked, "But Fred barely knows her."

Tommie put the plate on the table between their chairs. It's not a table, it's an old radio. If you slide the top open you can move the dials and push buttons, but no sound comes out. I think it was a radio a long time ago, like before there was television. That's called the olden days.

Wendy wanted some cookies. I dug around in the backpack. Wendy can't find things. She's good company, but not much help.

"Date squares!" Candi got up from her chair and limped over to take a square from the plate.

"It's because Fred's Catholic, not related by blood, plus he knew them the whole time," Tommie continued.

"Is he going to do it?" Mommy asked.

Wendy wondered what was taking me so long to find the cookies. I told her they were in the bottom of the bag and hard to find. She's unpatient.

Tommie said, "He doesn't have a choice, there's no one else who can."

"How many people do they need?" Mommy took up a date square and dabbed her cigarette in an ashtray. I went over to the date squares. I didn't know if I liked date squares. I poked one to see what they felt like. They were crumbly and soft.

"Take one or leave them alone," Mommy said. She always says stuff to me like I'm a little kid or something. There was mushy stuff in the middle. Date squares didn't look like they were good with tea. I went back and knelt on the blanket with Wendy.

"Are there raisins in these date squares?" Candi smooshed up her face while she held the date square up.

"Why can't they get a divorce?" Mommy asked.

Tommie pulled the mug from her lips and said, "She wants to get married again—in the Church."

I finally found two chocolate chip cookies in the backpack. I gave one to Wendy and one to me. Wendy thought they looked much better than date squares.

"Did she meet someone?" Mommy asked.

"Raisins ruin a date square," Candi said to me. Then she looked at Mommy and said, "Nell, did you put raisins in these date squares?"

"What?" Mommy's eyebrows went down like they do when I make a mess. Mommy hates people interrupting. "No, I only put in dates."

Wendy told me the chocolate chip cookies were great. She said Ashley and Holly would like them. We talked about the treehouse back home, and Wendy reminded me of when Ashley and me would push Holly and Wendy down the trunk like it was a slide in a playground. We didn't have tea in the treehouse because it was too hot, but Daddy or Mommy sometimes would bring us lemonade. Wendy hoped that they would still bring lemonade even without Ashley and Holly.

"It's putting Fred in a tough spot," Tommie said.

"Why? It's obviously over." Mommy said.

"Because he can't only say that it's over, he has to say it never happened."

"What does that mean: 'It never happened?'"

"To annul, the witnesses each have to declare to the Church that they were never truly married."

"What?!"

"They have to swear that the marriage bond never existed."

Mommy put down her mug. "But they were married for seven years . . . they have Jack!"

Grammy said Jack's coming to the cottage today. He's my cousin and nice. We went to visit him in California once, and he took me to the ocean, and we looked for shells. He caught a crab, and I could see its legs moving in the air. But he wasn't mean or anything, he showed me its belly, then put the crab back on the sand. It ran away super fast.

"That's the exercise, child or not," Tommie said.

Wendy got crumbs all over her. I used a paper napkin to dab her cheeks. I poured more tea into the teacups. Wendy asked what the adults were talking about. I told her they were talking about Jack's mom and dad and how they were going different ways. Wendy asked if Jack liked that or not.

"If the marriage never happened, is Jack a bastard?" Candi asked.

Tommie frowned. "First of all, you don't say 'bastard' anymore, you say 'illegitimate.' And second, it doesn't affect Jack's status because it's Canon law."

I pictured the big cannons at old Fort Henry. They get fired at New Year's. Ashley told me one of the soldiers had an accident once and lost his hand. It must have hurt a lot. I skinned my knee on one of the big rocks on the front lawn. That hurt, too. Wendy didn't like to think about broken hands. She asked me where Holly was moving to. I couldn't remember.

"Mommy?" I asked. "It's Mishi-something, right?"

Mommy stopped listening to Tommie, looked over at me, and asked, "What?"

"Mishynin? Myshikin?"

"Michigan, dear."

"How far away?"

"A thousand miles, dear."

Then I asked, "Do you want to play dolls with me?"

I knew the answer by Mom's eyebrow twitch.

"Not right now, dear. Maybe later."

Later meant never. Daddy was the one who played dolls with me. Mommy didn't like dolls. Sometimes she pretended, but you could tell she was thinking about work or her book club or where Daddy was.

Wendy asked if she could ride Buttercup. I opened the backpack and looked inside. Then I looked around the room. I told Wendy I would check upstairs. I had to walk past the adults to get to the stairs, but they were busy talking. I didn't think they saw me.

"It all seems so strange," Candi said.

"It's stupid," Mommy said, then looked over to where I had been sitting, two fingers on her lips. I was upstairs, but I still heard her whisper, "If you ask me."

I looked all over upstairs, in the beds, the dresser, on the floor, but I couldn't find Buttercup. I called down from the half wall that looked over the living room. "Mommy. Do you know where Buttercup is?"

"No," Mommy called back. "But he might be in the car."

I asked, "Can you get him for me?"

She looked up at me. "What do I look like, young lady, your maid?"

I thought for a second. Then I asked, "Can I go look?"

Mommy said, "Come here first. Let's feel your hands."

I slumped downstairs to take Mommy's outstretched hands. They felt warm and rough.

"You're still cold," she said, shaking her head. "You stay up late last night, and then you're in the lake for two hours this morning. You're going to make yourself sick."

"But the other kids were swimming, too," I said.

She didn't care.

"You're not shivery?" she asked, giving me her serious look that meant she thought I might not tell the truth.

"No."

"Well, go look in the car, but come right back."

"Okay." I was happy I could get away from the adults.

Candi asked, "Does Fred believe they never . . .?"

"Mommy?" I asked.

"What is it *now*?"

Because she was angry, I asked quietly, "Is the car door open?"

"I don't know," she answered. "The keys are on the hook above your father's bed if you need them." Mommy pointed to our picnic things and said, "But clean that up before you go."

I stacked the tea things, then placed them back in my pack. I folded up the blanket and put it with the backpack on the couch. I grabbed Wendy and carried her under my arm.

When I left the room, I heard Candi ask, "Maybe Fred can fudge it a bit?"

We went out the door into the backyard. On the back lawn, Aidan and Connor and the Doctor bent over a bucket.

I heard the Doctor ask, "Are you going to let it go?"

I wandered over to see what he was talking about. I looked in. A frog sat in the bottom of the bucket with an inch of water and some tufts of grass. I liked the frog's tiny hands and googly eyes. Then the frog jumped up against the side of the bucket, right at me. Wendy got scared and asked to leave.

I carried Wendy across the gravel road to the stones you step on through the grass. I went past the cabin up to the grass at the forest. Our car was parked in some mud under the trees. The car is big and green with a black roof, and it says "Ford LTD" on the side. I pressed the button for the back door, but I wasn't strong enough to open it with one hand. I put Wendy down and used two hands to press the button. Then the door opened. I grabbed Wendy, climbed up into the backseat, and closed the door.

The inside of our car was mainly black, with some silver. The baby's car seat with a pink blanket sat on the floor behind Daddy's seat. I always sat on the seat behind Mommy. On the drive here, I spilled orange juice on the floor, and somebody put muddy sandal prints on the back of Mommy's seat. Mommy hadn't seen either of these yet. I saw the stick from my Sugar Daddy poking out of the back pocket of Mommy's seat. I forgot I put it there. I peeled it out of the pocket where it had stuck to the material, had a few licks, then put it back for later. Wendy and I climbed into the front seats.

Kneeling on Daddy's seat, I could see over the dashboard out the front window. While Wendy watched from Mommy's seat,

I jiggled the arm for the windshield wipers, and the one for the turning lights. I moved the steering wheel back and forth, pulled the knob that turned on the headlights, and pressed the button for the cigarette lighter. When the lighter button popped, I pulled it out. The circle in the middle glowed orange. Ashley told me how much it hurt to touch the circle, so I didn't and put the lighter back in the hole.

Wendy moved over to Daddy's seat. She put on her sunglasses and fastened her seatbelt. I moved to the backseat and searched the rear window shelf: two colouring books, a scarf, one mitten, a box of Kleenex, some loose crayons and some crayons in a box, a deck of playing cards, and two stuffies. I pulled Buttercup out of the pile. He had on the brown saddle and matching bridle. His mane needed a comb, so I used my fingers. I looked at Wendy in the rear-view mirror and said, "I'm going to lie down here while you drive."

Wendy said that'd be okay.

I pulled the pink blanket from my sister's car seat and lay across the backseat. The blanket covered my shoulders, hips, and, if I bent my knees up all the way, my feet. I hugged Buttercup and shut my eyes. I didn't mean to fall asleep.

Jerry Flanagan knew lunch wouldn't be for at least an hour. Thickset, with a rolling bulldog-like gait, he was uncharacteristically scruffy-jawed in his favourite Coast Guard Academy T-shirt and red golf shorts as he made his way into the kitchen.

In the fridge he found some lettuce, mayonnaise, and leftover turkey. He combined these, along with a dash of salt and pepper, into a sandwich. He poured himself a glass of milk then walked out of the kitchen to the large dining table. Sitting at the end of the table, he ate half of the sandwich in three bites. As he bit into the other half, a voice called from the living room.

"Is that you, Jerry?"

"Mmmh?"

"Jerry?"

Swallowing, he answered, "Nell? What do you want?"

"Have you seen Esme?"

"She was swimming a while ago . . . but I sent her inside to get warm."

A snort came from the living room. "Yes, I know that. She was here. But she left to get one of her stuffies. She hasn't come back."

"Where'd she go?" Jerry asked.

"To the car." Nell leaned around the living room wall and issued a piercing stare at Jerry. "But that was a while ago."

"She probably found some cousins to play with. They're all outside."

"She was supposed to come right back here after getting the horse."

"Horse?"

"Yes, that was what she went for—her doll's horse."

Jerry took another bite of sandwich and a slurp of milk, which he realized likely didn't score him any points with Nell, then asked, "Should I go look for her?"

"Could you? We're discussing what to do about Patrick." Her head disappeared around the corner.

Jerry didn't want to get dragged into the Patrick affair. He finished his sandwich, gulped the remainder of his milk, then confirmed, "She went to the car?"

"Yes. Tell her to come back inside. She needs to warm up. We don't want her sick again."

"She might have found something else to do."

Nell craned her neck around the corner again. "Do I need to go?"

He knew the correct answer.

"I'm off," he called rising from the table.

He deposited his dishes in the kitchen sink, wiped his mouth, and went out the back door into bright sunshine. On the back lawn, Jerry saw the Doctor with two kids leaning over a bucket.

"What'cha got there?" he asked.

"A frog." Aidan answered. "It's a green frog, not a bullfrog, 'cuz its ears are smaller."

"That's a good-looking frog. What're ya going do with it?" Jerry asked.

"We're gonna watch him for a bit and then take him back down the pond and let him go," Connor said.

"Yeah," Aidan added. "The Doctor says we can't let him go here. It's too far to the pond and he might not make it."

Jerry cub-saluted the two boys and turned to head up toward the forest.

"Good luck!" he called over his shoulder.

As he crossed the gravel road, Jerry pulled a toothpick from his pocket to loosen a piece of lettuce from between his front teeth. He continued to the back of the property, where the Doctor had his vegetable garden. He took a few moments to inspect the carrots, the beans, and the potatoes, then tossed his toothpick into the forest and sauntered over to the car.

Through the windshield, he saw a standing doll belted into the driver's seat. The doll's hand was positioned on the steering wheel, her head turned slightly as if about to make a left turn. He recognized his daughter's attention to detail.

Esme lay on the backseat, clutching a toy horse, asleep. Her feet stuck out from under the baby's blanket.

A few weeks ago, she had walked home, by herself, from the swimming pool. Nell had had a conniption, but all Jerry could think, with a sense of mingled pride and sorrow, was how grown-up his daughter was getting. He watched the freckles on her nose move with her breathing and remembered playing connect the dots with her and one of Nell's makeup pencils. When Esme went into the kitchen and Nell saw her face, both he and Esme got in trouble.

With a start, Esme looked up. Her initial confusion turned to a smile of recognition.

"Daddy!"

He opened the door, "How are you, Miss Moo?"

"Daddy! I told you not to call me that anymore. It's embarrassing!"

She sat up.

"What'cha doing here?" Jerry asked, sitting down beside her.

"I came to get Wendy's horse, but I fell asleep. By accident."

Gently, he took the horse and looked it over, nodding appreciatively. He checked its saddle and its bridle. He tugged on one of its legs, felt along its chest and inspected the horse's feet and teeth, imitating judges he had seen on a TV dog show. Esme watched, fascinated.

"Beautiful horse." He handed it back to Esme. "Does it have a name?"

"Buttercup."

"Of course," he banged his knuckles on his head. "Buttercup. I knew that didn't I?"

Esme smiled, "Yes. You just forgot."

"Where's Wendy driving?"

"We're going home."

"Did you forget something?"

"No. Wendy wants to go sit in the treehouse and drink lemonade."

"That sounds fun," Jerry said. "But can't you do that after we visit at the lake?"

Esme shook her head. "We have to go now."

"I thought it was fun here—swimming, canoeing, playing with your cousins?"

"Yeah, that's fun," she said. "And I like Grammy and the Doctor and the doughnuts."

"Then why do you want to go home?"

"It's not me," she explained. "It's Wendy. She doesn't like it here as much anymore."

Jerry said, "I see. Did she used to like it here?"

"Yes. She liked it when there was roast marshmallows and jumping off the dock contests and the singsongs. And she liked the duck family—I fed the ducklings!"

"When was that?"

"Grammy let us throw breadcrumbs to them this morning. They all came over to eat. Two even bumped into each other!" She giggled.

"Did Wendy see it?"

"No. She was asleep on the bed. She missed the ducklings and the swimming and Scottie jumping off the dock."

"Maybe that's why she wants to go? She's missing the fun?"

Esme shook her head, "No. That's not it. She's having fun."

"If she's having fun, why go home?"

Esme tugged on Buttercup's halter then flicked his bridle back and forth. She stroked Buttercup's mane a few times before looking up. "Holly moved away at the end of school."

"Holly?"

"You know, Ashley's doll," Esme explained. "Holly and Wendy did everything together. They were best friends. But Holly left."

"The family moved to Michigan, didn't they?"

"Yes," Esme answered.

"But what's that got to do with Grand Lake?" Jerry asked.

"Well, there's that, and then there's Uncle Patrick's not going to be Jack's dad anymore."

"What?" Jerry asked, shaking his head. "Who told you that?"

"It's supposed to be a secret. Patrick and Christine are getting an L and they won't be married."

"An 'L'?"

"That's what Mommy said. Their marriage is getting an L, so they won't even have been married and Patrick and Christine won't have bonds of marriage and . . . something."

Jerry put his arm around Esme's shoulder. "But Uncle Patrick will still be Jack's dad."

"Christine won't be his mom?" she asked.

"Christine will still be Jack's mom. Pat will still be Jack's dad. But they won't be married to each other anymore."

Esme looked down at her blanket, saying nothing. Jerry looked out the side window. A wind had kicked up around the car. The leaves in the trees overhead rustled. A paper bag flew up into the forest, bouncing off tree trunks until it passed from view. They sat together watching.

Esme tugged on his shirt, "Jack will still have a dad and a mom?"

"Yes."

She brushed Buttercup's mane a few times and stroked his tail. "And Wendy might get a new friend?"

"You bet she will."

"And I might be able to go visit Ashley in Michigan?"

"Only if I can go, too."

Esme held Buttercup up over her head touching his nose to the roof of the car. Without taking her eye off the horse, she asked, "Daddy?"

"Uh huh?"

"I'll always get to stay with you and Mommy, right?"

Jerry looked out the window and into the forest. He was quiet. Esme cantered Buttercup along the car seat until he reached the door.

"Daddy?"

Jerry turned and he gazed at her, a constriction formed behind his forehead that crawled down into his chest. He knew some part of her had seen and some part might have understood even before he had. He recognized the inevitable crush of experience, felt his powerlessness to stave it off. Emotion and helplessness clogged his throat.

"Daddy!" She dropped Buttercup and grabbed his hand. Her hands were soft, pink, and cool.

He willed himself to smile and nod and say as if it was truth, "Mommy and I will always be there together for you, Miss Moo. Don't you worry."

The tension on her face dissipated into belief. He had given her that, at least. She punched his arm lightly and smiled up at him. "I told you not to call me that."

She rolled onto his chest, put her arms over his shoulders, and buried her face in his neck. As she hung there, he felt a warm wet spot spread through his shirt onto his shoulder. He sat in the backseat, still, watching the beans in the garden sway in the breeze and the shadows moving from spot to dappled spot until a cardinal swooped across his vision, waking him from this reverie. He looked down at his daughter. It was time to get back.

"Can Wendy ride Buttercup?"

Esme spoke into his neck, "She's been practising."

"Can I see?"

She pulled back. "Sure! Do you want to come for a picnic with us?"

"Will there be corn on the cob?"

"Okay!" Esme grabbed Wendy from the front seat. "But the picnic stuff's back in the cottage."

"Race you there!" Jerry opened the car door.

They sprinted across the grass toward the back door. Halfway there, Jerry grabbed Esme, lifted her up onto his back, and carried her the rest of the way to the cottage.

Through the kitchen window, a willowy figure in curlers inhales on a cigarette. She watches her husband carry her daughter on his back. She crushes her cigarette in a coffee can on the counter, exhaling the last dregs of smoke. As the two burst through the door, gasping and laughing, she turns to see if there is any more coffee.

SHAYNE: PIGGYBACK

Once the boys disappear with their bucket, I root around in my bag for a book. I pull out *Danger on the Vampire Trail*, my favourite. I've got like twenty Hardy Boys books 'cuz I buy a new one as soon as I've saved up enough from allowances. It's easy to get lost in the world of teenage detectives and forget what's going on around you. Frank and Joe are only a few years older than me, but they have the best life. They chase down bad guys, stay up late, play a bunch of sports, and don't seem to worry about adults much. I'd like to be a detective when I grow up, or at least write stories about detectives.

I get to the part of the book where Frank and Joe are driving down the highway to go camping, when a man and the girl with the doll come running down from behind the cabin. They seem to be racing each other, but it's obvious the man—he must be her dad—isn't running as hard as he can. Plus, the girl runs like a little kid: arms and legs all over the place, not giving a hoot about form. The man doesn't seem to care either, which is odd for an adult. They sprint past the cabin, across the grass, and she keeps looking back at him, laughing. I worry she's going to trip or something, but she doesn't. When she gets to the dirt road, he grabs her, pops her up onto his back. She squeals. He runs beside the cottage down toward the lake with her piggyback.

They have no idea I saw them. The good thing is, they don't care. I like it when people do what makes them happy and don't care what other people think, even if they look kind of goofy. Especially when they look goofy.

When I was a little kid, I loved going to the Eaton's Santa Claus Parade. It was usually freezing cold. Mom'd only come on the years it was warmer. Dad and I'd get bundled up, hop on the subway, and head down to the Museum station. Outside the museum you could smell roasting nuts and sweet burnt sugar. It came from this guy with a wood and glass cart who sold cotton candy. He'd have chestnuts roasting and popcorn. Dad'd get us a couple of hot chocolates and a bag of roasted nuts to share. Then we'd stand outside the museum, eating chestnuts, sipping our drinks, waiting for the parade to go by. There'd be tons of people everywhere when the parade finally started, with some old guy in a business suit sitting in a car, waving at everyone. The last float was always Santa, and he'd throw candy canes at the crowd. Once you got a candy cane, the parade was basically over. We went year after year. It was always the same, and maybe because I knew what was going to happen, it was always fun.

One year, Dad suggested we walk along with the parade instead of watching it flow past us. I wasn't too sure at first. We didn't get in trouble or anything, but you aren't supposed to walk along with the parade, it's supposed to walk past you. No one seemed to care that we were walking with the parade. Instead of getting angry with us, people started waving at us—like we were part of the parade.

We followed this giant float with a dragon on it. Beside the float was a bunch of people wearing robes and singing church music. Then this tall guy in a black cape who stood on the dragon float invited us to walk beside it, and we were in the parade. It's different being in a parade than watching a parade. You hear whistles and people clapping from the sides, and there are clowns darting back and forth everywhere handing out pinwheels. Everyone's looking at you. You're not watching everything flow by; you're in the middle of it. The people watching expect you to do something, at least wave at them and smile.

At first, I got super excited about being in the parade, but after a while I got tired of all the waving and the smiling.

"I wanna stop, Dad."

He looked at me like I was crazy. "Stop! We can't stop. We might never get to do this again."

"But my feet hurt." I admit I was a bit whiney, but as a kid you only have so many tools.

He stopped for a second and put a finger up. "I'll carry you!"

"Carry me?" I asked.

"You know, piggyback." He stooped down. I could tell he wanted to stay with the parade. He'd get excited about stuff like that. With him carrying me, I figured I could keep going. Plus, getting a piggyback is always fun.

"Okay," I said. I climbed up on his back.

Dad carried me the rest of the parade route. He had to put me down once, but only for a minute, and even when he put me down, he didn't let go of me.

Back then, I thought he'd never let me go.

THE FORT

Rory read a book about bears. Reading about bears hadn't made him comfortable with bears. Rory didn't like bears.

Rory didn't like being in the forest.

Rory didn't like being alone.

Yet, here he was, alone, in the forest, watching for . . . well, he didn't know for what. He was watching. The others said they would be back, that it would not take long, but even when they said it, he wasn't convinced. Already it seemed like a long time. He was thirsty and getting tired.

Standing there.

In the forest.

Guarding a fort.

It was a good fort. Wooden walls tied together with rawhide and duct tape, windows cut out of one side, two sheets of overlapping corrugated aluminum for a roof. Inside, an old bookshelf sat at one end. Some chairs—two with broken legs— were scattered along the sides. An old indoor-outdoor carpet covered two thirds of the floor and a blue tarpaulin the last third. A large wire spool table was littered with comic books, two intact battle chestnuts, a bag of marshmallows taken from the kitchen, and a jug of chocolate milk missing its lid.

This was the fort they asked him to guard. He wasn't sure what from. They hadn't been specific. He hadn't asked the right questions—any questions, really. They had invited him to come to their fort, something they'd never done before. He wasn't going to ask too many questions. That he would be left behind in the fort, in the forest, hadn't occurred to him. But when they got here, the others explained that he was the newest member of the club and had to guard the fort while the others went on the expedition.

So, here he was, standing, listening, watching. He was sure they would be back soon. They wouldn't leave him alone in the forest, not for too long. It's not like he had seen or heard anything to guard against. Not yet anyway. He could see trees, a few birds, lots of bugs, and he'd counted seventeen toadstools from where he stood. He'd like to see them up close, maybe even touch them. What he didn't want to see, or touch, was a big animal. Especially not a bear.

Before they left, they had given him a hockey stick.

The hockey stick was made of wood, and he could swing it back and forth. But as a weapon against a bear, he could see a few problems, the most obvious being that to use the hockey stick against a bear, he would need to get close to the bear. More precisely, he would have to be less than the hockey stick's length away from the bear. And, in looking at the stick again, it didn't seem to Rory that the hockey stick was all that long. It seemed kind of short. Like it was for a little kid. He wondered whether they had left him with only a kid's hockey stick to guard the fort against a bear. Probably not, but he wasn't sure. Rory didn't play hockey.

He'd got a book from the school library about bears. The book had said that bears feared humans. If that was true, then any encounter he had with a bear would be terrifying for both him and the bear. But, he imagined, mostly him. If a bear came at him, and he had to use the hockey stick, he'd have to get close enough to smell the bear's breath, feel the bear's fur, hear the bear's growls. Even with a hockey stick, he didn't like his chances. Not even with a good swing. The book about bears said a bear's skin was thick, their skulls were hard, and they were fast. Even if he somehow managed to hit the bear with the stick, he wasn't going to stop the bear.

Maybe if he yelled or whistled as loud as he could.

He could whistle loud. Kids at school said it hurt their ears, his whistle. They'd asked him to teach them how to whistle like he could: not using his fingers. But their front teeth didn't overlap, so the way he whistled wouldn't work for them.

But a bear? The book said bears either didn't have good hearing or didn't have good vision. He couldn't remember which it was, exactly when it would be handy to know. If bears didn't hear well, then a loud whistle wouldn't be much help. He'd be back to nothing but the hockey stick.

He could always run. Rory could run fast. Maybe not as fast as a bear, but fast for an eight-year-old. It wasn't that far to the cottage, if he saw a bear. That'd be the sensible thing to do. The Doctor warned everyone to get in the cottage if they saw a bear. It was the Doctor's cottage. He should know. The bear wouldn't come inside. But Matt said that on no account should Rory leave the fort. Rory had asked why, but Matt asked him whether he wanted to be part of the club or not. That was after Matt said they would be 'right back.'

Where were they, anyway? He was starving. It was bologna sandwiches and chips for lunch. His favourite. After cheeseburgers and pizza . . . and those pocket things Mom got from the Indian grocer. Okay, so his fourth favourite, but still. Maybe that's where they were: at lunch, eating all the sandwiches and chips while they left him stuck in the forest. They were probably laughing at him. Like at school, where he was sure they laughed at him, behind his back. Everyone was nice to his face, but he knew. One day he would walk into the cafeteria or the gym or homeroom when they weren't expecting him, and he'd catch them at it. Laughing at his crooked teeth, or his head gear, or his stutter.

Or they'd all be aliens.

Or bears.

He had a theory that other people were aliens or animals in disguise. They'd change back into their actual form when he wasn't around. He'd tried to sneak up on other people a couple of times, but they must have heard him or seen him.

It had to be lunchtime by now.

At least if he knew where the bear was, he could prepare. Plan something. Not knowing if there was one and not knowing where it was and not knowing even what kind of bear it was . . . well, he had read about bears.

There was a big dark, round, lump through the trees. It hadn't moved, but bears hibernated sometimes. If it was hibernating, it wasn't going to attack him. That was good. Except it wasn't winter. The book said bears hibernated in winter. They slept in a cave or the base of an old tree. Whatever he could see through the trees wasn't a hibernating bear. He'd read that after months of hibernating, bears came out hungry—starving—ready to eat. Anything. Maybe even skinny boys with hockey sticks.

TOOWITTOOWOO.

Rory started, stumbled, and almost dropped the hockey stick. Stupid bird!

Where *were* those guys? How long would he have to guard this fort?

The lump was still under that tree. Had it moved? He squinted through the trees and shafts of sunlight, trying to get a better view. The forest was dark and creepy and full of noises. All he could do was watch and listen and hope the others'd be back soon.

He watched.

And listened.

He heard something.

"Rowrrrreee!"

A growl? What exactly did a bear's growl sound like? The book said they growled, but didn't really describe the sound. Not much help if you don't know what a bear's growl sounded like. Ms. Rowntree, who lived three doors down from Rory's family, had a Yorkshire terrier, Buster, who growled every time Rory tried to scratch his ears, but the growl was kind of funny, because Buster was tiny, and he shook when he growled. An animal who shakes when it growls isn't scary. A bear probably doesn't shake when it growls. A bear's growl is going to be scarier than a Yorkshire terrier's growl. An imprecise word: growl.

"Rowrrrreee!"

That could be a growl. It might not be. But whatever it was, it was getting closer.

He thought maybe the lump was getting bigger too. Moving toward the fort.

Maybe.

It was hard to see in the forest. It was either too dark in the shade, or too bright where the sun broke through the branches. Shadows shifted, came, and went. Not ideal for spotting movement.

He saw—a head?—poke up from the lump. Then maybe a limb waving in the air. Or was it a branch? Rory gripped the hockey stick, holding it up high, so the blade hovered over his shoulder. He wanted to be sure whatever it was could see the hockey stick, that Rory was serious. He planted his feet in the doorway of the fort and told himself he wasn't afraid.

He took a deep breath. Squeezed the shaft of the hockey stick. Bent his knees.

"Rory!" it bellowed.

He turned and ran—through the trees, over brush and roots, trampling shrubs, breaking toadstools, making a beeline to the cottage. He didn't care what Matt thought. He didn't care about the fort. He didn't want to be part of a stupid club.

Rory read a book about bears. The book hadn't said anything about bears who waved at you. It hadn't said anything about bears that called your name.

Rory needed a better book.

SHAYNE: SANDWICHES

The Doctor comes across the lawn carrying two plates.

"Lunch?" he calls out as he gets near the car.

Through the window, he hands me a plate with a sandwich, chips, and pickles. Then he sits in one of the metal chairs on the lawn. The chair has a clamshell back which, because its paint is flaking off, I can tell used to be brown, but someone spraypainted it yellow. I take a bite of the sandwich and realize how hungry I am. Even though it's only a bologna sandwich, it tastes awesome. I eat the chips and even the pickles.

"Thanks!" I call out the window. "This is great."

"I can't eat this second one." He holds up his plate, his hand shaking a bit. "You want it?"

"Sure!"

He comes over, passes the sandwich through the window, and goes back to his chair. While I eat, he gazes up into the forest, occasionally using his fingers to comb back what's left of his thin, grey hair. I can hear him humming to himself as he sits there. Mom does the same thing. If she's in the kitchen or sewing or folding laundry, and thinks no one is around, she sings to herself. Supposedly it's crazy people who talk to themselves, but I don't get a crazy vibe from him, or from her. Plus, Dad never did it.

But you're not supposed to say 'crazy.'

"I slept in a car once," the Doctor says through the window. "We were in Ireland. A rental car. We arrived late at night, got the car from the airport, but were too late and our hotel had closed for the night, and we couldn't check in. Grammy and I were tired. We pulled over to the side of the road—they drive on the other side there—and went to sleep. Didn't have a choice. A policeman woke us up in the morning."

"Police?"

"Yeah, a huge guy. He'd have been scary if he was chasing you. He tapped his stick on our window and said good morning. Grammy was a bit flustered and began to explain how we'd come to be sleeping in a car on a Dublin street, but he put up his hand to stop her, tipped his hat, and continued his patrol."

"Maybe he thought you were lost."

"Maybe. It wasn't the most comfortable sleep I've ever had, but when we finally got into the hotel, the shower was hot, the bed was soft, and they had a nice breakfast set out. It was wonderful. Sometimes a bit of discomfort reminds you to appreciate what you have taken for granted."

There might be some kernel of wisdom he's trying to pass along, or maybe he gets a kick out of thinking about that policeman and telling the story. I can't figure out which it is, plus I keep staring at the mustard smear on the corner of his mouth. I betcha Jesus or Buddha sometimes got mustard on the corner of their mouth while they were telling their sermons, and when they did, I bet whatever they were talking about that day didn't get recorded by anyone trying to listen because it's distracting when the person telling you a story has something on their face.

Eventually, I tap the corner of my mouth to show him where the mustard is. He takes the tip of his finger, wipes off the patch, then pops the finger in his mouth.

"Thanks," he says. He uses the wet tip of his finger to dab up the chip crumbs on his plate.

I'm almost finished the second sandwich when this skinny kid comes barrelling out of the forest. He's yelling and waving a hockey stick in the air as he passes. He looks scared, or a bit insane. A part of me wonders if maybe he's been lost up in the woods for a couple of days or something.

"Rory!" the Doctor stands and tries to stop him, but Rory runs right by, across the road, over the lawn, bangs open the cottage door and darts inside.

After he disappears, the Doctor turns to look at me. At first, neither of us says or does anything, unsure what happened. Then he chuckles and says, "There's a story there."

"Where's he coming from?"

"Probably from the fort. Up in the woods. The kids built it last week. Looks like something spooked him up there."

"There's a fort?" I peer into the forest but can't see any fort.

The Doctor stands up, comes to the window of the car, and says, "I'll show it to you sometime."

He takes my plate and heads back down to the cottage, stopping along the way to examine a blue dragonfly that has landed on the picnic table.

I get into my sleeping bag and open my book. That Rory kid was having a rough day. Some days are like that. You can't tell when the rough days are going to come, but you've still gotta get through them. Life'd be easier if it was a Hardy Boys book. The answer to what's happening would be revealed at the perfect moment. All you'd have to do is hang on until then. Everything'd be easier, if you knew someone was gonna tell you the answer when you need it.

Dad thought I read too many Hardy Boys books. He called them "juvenile" and kept trying to get me to read something else.

"What about a pirate story like *Treasure Island*, or science fiction like *Twenty Thousand Leagues Under the Sea*? I'll even buy it for you."

But Frank and Joe Hardy felt like family. Some pirate guy with a black spot that kills him for some reason a million years ago in language I don't understand wasn't the same. But because he insisted the books were great, I gave them a try. I didn't mind *Old Yeller* until the end when I cried. And that Holden Caulfield guy I kinda liked, especially the part where he takes off and shouts 'so long' to the morons at the school. I totally get that, and I didn't even go to his school. But for the most part, Dad's books didn't click with me. It was great he liked them, but I kept coming back to the Hardy Boys. They felt comfortable, which is what you want sometimes. Like now.

The Doctor reappears. He walks over to the clothesline between the shed and the tree and grabs a towel.

"Interested in a swim?" he asks.

I shake my head. "No thanks."

"Maybe tomorrow." He calls out over his shoulder and saunters past the car, across the road and down to the lake. He starts singing again. His voice echoes up the path even after he has passed from sight.

I took to the woods to find some peace
From the hustle and bustle of city streets
The wind whistled through the trees in song
Those branches told me life on earth is not long

The song kinda gets to me. It makes me think of those two extra seconds. Not a lot of extra time, but you should try to use them for something. It makes me wonder if, maybe, I should be doing something other than sitting in this car.

If he sang that song on purpose, which I'm not saying he did, the old Doc is a smart one. He never bosses you, or guilts you, or threatens you. He gets you thinking.

Then again, maybe he was just singing a song.

ABSENT DRAKE

A pale sun shines through the dissipating clouds. From the grass at the side of the beach, Finn watches a sandpiper stick its long beak into the sand and pull something out. The piper tilts its head up then shakes what it caught down its throat. While the piper combs the sand, Finn tosses rocks at an abandoned sandal, knocking it closer to the water each time he hits it.

From the docks to his right, Finn hears Matt, who lives on the beach and already has lip hair, say, "You got a bunch of loonies living at your camp."

"Like who?" Dylan asks.

"You got that stupid kid sitting in the car. What's his problem? Sitting there watching from the back of a car . . . makes me wanna punch him."

"You mean Shayne?" Liam says.

"I don't know what his name is, and I don't care. He's weird. Then there's the Doctor, always humming to himself, sticking his nose in everywhere. Worst of all, there's that uncle of yours who mumbles a lot and stares off into space all the time."

Finn stops tossing the rocks to listen.

"He probably poops himself! If my dad was like that I'd run away."

Matt stands a head taller than Dylan and Liam. When Matt laughs, the roll under his chin vibrates. "Did you hear him at lunch? Going on about what the Pope told him? Cuckoo if you ask me."

"Yeah," says Liam, laughing. "He kept trying to ask Mac how Lily was doing. And she's dead."

Dylan shakes his head, "His claw hands scare me."

"He's your uncle. You might get it," Matt says.

"Get it?" Liam asks.

"If you spend too much time around him, you get it, too. At least I live down here on the beach."

The sandpiper darts away through the grass.

"You can't catch it," Liam says.

"That's what they want you to think. So, you'll be nice and all. They don't wanna put him in the loonie bin 'cuz they feel sorry for him." Matt crouches. Finn's cousins move in closer. Finn strains to hear. "But if it was me, I wouldn't touch him or nothing . . . in fact, I probably shouldn't get too near you!" Matt backs away. "You probably've touched him already."

The two shake their heads.

"Not me!"

"Not me!"

Matt stands and squints at them. "Why should I believe you? You're in the same cottage. You might've touched him accidentally."

"No!" Dylan says. "I don't go anywhere near him. I don't want him to drool on me."

"Me neither."

"You sure?"

They nod.

"Pinkie swear?" Matt asks.

Matt holds out his right pinkie. Dylan and Liam hold out their bent fingers. The three join. They shout, "I swear!" and spit over their left shoulders.

Finn's hand closes over a rock.

The sun is now high and warm. Finn sits alone on the concrete retaining wall, his legs dangling over the water. The front door of the cottage opens, then bangs shut. Finn turns at the sound, wipes his eyes, and watches the Doctor cross the grass to the dock.

The Doctor has swim trunks on and carries a towel over his shoulder. He places the towel and his wire-rimmed glasses on a lawn chair and stubs his cigarette in the dirt at the bottom of the boathouse wall. He walks to the end of the dock and bends down to dip his toe in the water.

Over his shoulder the Doctor calls, "You coming?"

Finn freezes. The Doctor looks right at him.

"Coming?" Finn asks.

"For a swim? We'll go down to the beach."

"Uh . . ." Finn leans forward to look left, down to the beach.

"We'll swim slowly."

Finn hesitates.

"Have you ever swum to the beach?" the Doctor asks.

Finn shakes his head.

"How about to the float?" The Doctor points to the middle of the bay.

"I swam there once."

"It's only a bit further. You just keep swimming." The Doctor climbs down the small ladder at the side of the dock.

Finn looks down into the water. He wipes his eyes again.

"Let's see a cannonball," the Doctor says.

Finn looks over at the dock.

"Your best one, now!" the Doctor calls from the water.

Finn stands, shuffles over to the start of the dock and takes off his shirt. He takes a deep breath, sprints, and leaps off the end, aiming for the rooftops across the lake. For a moment he hangs above the water. Then he plunges, shattering the still surface.

"How old are you?" the Doctor asks after Finn bobs back up.

"Nine."

"Nine! I thought you must be at least twelve with a cannonball like that."

"I'm big for my age," Finn offers.

The Doctor glides away from the dock. He stretches and scissor kicks.

Sidestroke, Finn thinks. Pluck the flower, put it in the basket. They taught him that in swim lessons. Mom makes him go.

Finn swims after his grandfather.

"That's the Hannigan place," the Doctor says as they glide past a blue and grey cottage. "They've been on the lake almost as long as we have. Suzie Hannigan used to teach fifth grade up in Woodstock."

Finn wonders if Ms. Hannigan whistles when she says the letter S, like his fifth-grade teacher, Ms. Jarvis.

"The green and yellow one is the Hoyts' cottage. Your mom and Dan Hoyt were going to practise medicine together."

"What happened?" Finn asks.

"Your mom got accepted to a different university and that was it."

"It?" Finn stops swimming.

"She met your dad at university. Head over heels—poor Dan didn't know what hit him, or her. I'm not sure your mom knew either."

"My dad?"

"Yup. The next summer they were engaged. The summer after that they were married, then you came along."

The Doctor glides off.

Finn takes another look at the green and yellow cottage, then follows his grandfather. The water feels cool. He swims past a spinney of trees partly hiding a red and white cottage. His friend Jessie lives there, but she's gone to Houlton for the day.

"What was Dad like then?" Finn asks as he glides along beside the Doctor.

The Doctor takes four or five long strokes, then answers, "He could play cribbage better than anyone. A terrible golfer, but he loved to play. The first morning he got here, he jumped off the dock and swam out to Blueberry Point, because he could. Then he swam back and made pancakes and bacon for everyone. By that point, I think even Grammy was in love with him."

Finn smiles. "He's a good swimmer."

They swim steadily, past the yellow cottage where Finn never sees anyone, and a white cottage that has people on the weekends, but no kids. The shore here is rock and trees. Getting in and out of the water is hard. A couple of days ago, he tried to climb out on one of the rocks but slipped, cutting his knee open. He'd howled until help came. The Doctor cleaned the cut and put pink spray on it. The spray stung a little, but it also felt nice and cool and marked you as an injured person for the rest of the day. Finn got to drink warm, sweet tea and eat a cookie to help him get better.

"I see you swimming with him in the mornings," the Doctor says.

"Yeah," Finn sputters, swallowing water, "we like to go first thing. He's better in the mornings when no one's around. We can talk a bit. He likes to fish, too. It's good when we're alone."

"He probably doesn't like the crowd here."

"It isn't always bad. You can tell from his hands when he's not happy."

"That's the medication," the Doctor explains.

"Yeah, Mom told me that, but I wish it didn't."

"Why?"

"That's usually how people know—his hands." Finn's cheeks feel warm, but the water is cool on his neck.

"Is that bad?" the Doctor asks.

"I don't care." Finn takes three hard, fast strokes. "But people look at him funny . . . think they know him. If Dad's quiet and sitting still or reading a book they can't tell. It's his hands, or when he talks to himself, that people see it."

They come across a family of ducks paddling in and out of the rocks, five ducklings close to their mother. Finn stops swimming and treads water. The duck moves smoothly, while the ducklings herk and jerk and spin behind their mother, unsure how to steer. They try to dive but barely get half of their fuzzy bodies under the surface before popping up again.

"They won't stay small for long," the Doctor muses. "By the fall, they'll be big enough to fly south and escape the winter."

Finn swims. The water parts and burbles over his fingers at each stroke. He watches a small wake ripple from his front hand back across the surface to the shore. Pockets of cool water and then pockets of warm water envelop his shoulders and chest. Danny said that the warmer water is where fish peed. Mom said that was only a fish story and laughed. Finn laughed with her, not knowing whether she was laughing at Danny's story or at what she had said. It was always hard to tell with her.

"When you came along, he couldn't stop talking about you. Your first word, your first step, your first swimming lesson. As if he were the only man who had ever become a dad, and wanted to share the whole experience with the unfortunate people who weren't as lucky."

Finn doesn't remember this, but he remembers playing catch and Dad teaching him to skate and letting him jump off the high diving board when Mom wasn't watching. Great bear hugs and tickle spider and sharing midnight hot chocolate with sugar cookies when Finn couldn't sleep.

"I remember him. What he was like," Finn says.

"It's important that you do."

Then, afraid to get an answer, but more afraid not to, Finn asks, "But where's he gone?"

He can feel the Doctor thinking about how to respond and hopes that he will—that finally someone will.

"He's still there," the Doctor says. "I see him when you play near him, especially when you laugh. I see it when your mother holds his hand or plays with his hair."

Finn's face trembles. He knows the lake water isn't hiding his tears, but he doesn't care.

"I know he is. I just wish—" Finn kicks away toward the beach.

When at last they reach the beach, the Doctor leaves the water to sit in the sand. His bronzed skin sags off the bone, wrinkly and wet. His arms and legs are almost the same skinny thickness. His feet are calloused from walking around without shoes—he never wears shoes, even to drive—and Finn can see that his toenails are broken and yellowing.

After a few minutes pretending to look for fish and clams in the shallows, Finn wanders over to sit beside the Doctor. Shouts from the public beach carry across the water. Laughter and squeals and hollers bombard Finn until some part of him finally gives way. The Doctor puts his arm on Finn's shoulder but says nothing.

Finn leans against his grandfather. He feels mad and sad but likes that he isn't being asked to explain.

When Finn finally sits up, he is tired but somehow lighter. He shivers despite the heat.

"Is that what happened this morning?" the Doctor asked.

Finn looks down at the sand.

"What'd they say?" asks the Doctor.

"They didn't know I was there," Finn says, still staring at the sand.

"But what did Matt say?"

Finn writes in the sand with his finger.

"He made them swear not to touch, that Dad might be contagious . . . Matt's a big jerk, and maybe I shouldn't have thrown the rock, but Dad still hears everything. You can't act like he isn't even there. Like he has no feelings."

"They don't understand. They're kids," the Doctor tries to explain.

"So am I," Finn says. "And he's my dad."

The Doctor looks down at his hand, nodding.

They sit together watching the lake.

After a while the Doctor rises to his feet and asks, "Wanna walk back?"

"Let's swim and see the ducks again," Finn says.

"You sure you're up to it?"

Finn runs into the water.

They swim past the rocky shore and the cottages hidden in the trees until they come to the front of Mac's place. The ducklings appear. Finn and the Doctor stop to watch them. The sun is warm, and the water is cool. Finn's cousins shout at each other up in the forest. He tries to see what they are doing, but he is too low in the water. He hears a splash and a quack behind him.

The ducklings beetle through the water toward their mother. They dodge around her until she gives a loud quack and turns to paddle toward the beach, ducklings in tow.

Finn and his grandfather swim back to the dock and climb out. A big red towel is draped across one of the chairs by the boathouse. Finn's shirt rests on the towel. He drags his toes across the grass a couple of times to get the sand from the steps off, then wraps himself in the red towel and pulls on his shirt.

"Thanks for the swim," Finn calls to his grandfather. He wraps himself tighter in the towel then heads into the cottage.

In the living room, a gaunt, frail-looking man lolls in an armchair, a blanket tucked around his legs. The TV is on, but he isn't looking at it. His legs bounce to a rhythm Finn can't hear. Finn walks through the cottage into the kitchen. He starts the kettle and gets out two mugs. He takes two pouches of hot chocolate mix and, when the kettle roils, adds water and the mix to each cup.

Finn carries the two mugs from the kitchen, through the dining room and back into the living room. He goes over, puts one of the mugs on the table beside the man and the other on the floor. He sits cross-legged at the man's feet and looks at the TV screen the man isn't watching.

"The Doctor and I went swimming," Finn says. "I made it all the way to the beach . . . I did sidestroke mostly . . . a couple of times I had to stop, but I didn't touch bottom."

Finn turns to see if the man is listening. The man's aspect is unchanged.

"There were ducklings. They swam back and forth. Sometimes they dove under the water. I saw a couple of them eating weeds. They looked happy. Maybe next time we go swimming we could head down to the beach and look for the ducklings, then you can see them too?"

Finn thinks about the ducklings as he watches the man. The man's thumb and ring finger on both hands press together hard enough that the man's hands shake. Finn quietly stands, takes the man's hands in his and smooths them out with gentle stroking. He asks simply, "Okay?'

When he lets go, the man's hands rest folded in his lap.

"The ducklings were with their mother. She watched them, pointed them where to go, showed them what to eat, then led them down to the beach."

Finn looks into the man's eyes. This man, who sits in a chair. This man, who doesn't answer him. May not even recognize him. This man stares at something Finn can't see and listens to sounds Finn can't hear. Finn, wrapped in a red towel, turns to the TV screen. He leans back, resting against his father's legs.

"I liked the ducklings, and I liked the duck. But I kept thinking . . ." Finn turned to look up at the man. "You know what I kept thinking?"

The man in the chair doesn't answer.

"I kept thinking: Where's the drake?"

SHAYNE: MOM AND MATT

It's the middle of the afternoon, and clouds have rolled across the sky to dampen the heat. The cicadas have stopped buzzing, and there is a smell of damp in the air.

"Everything okay?" Mom asks, approaching the car with a pair of garden shears and a bunch of daisies in her hand.

I put down the Hardy Boys, nod, and give her a thumbs up, hoping she'll leave me alone.

"Do you want to talk? Or play cards?"

I shake my head. "I'm good."

"Is there anything I can do? Anything at all?"

I shake my head again.

I think she is going to leave, but instead she sits on a tree stump beside the toolshed, watching me, the knuckles on her left hand betraying how hard she is grasping the flowers.

I know I worry her. I wish I didn't, but I understand why she is worried about her kid. The fact that she worries is comforting, in a demented sort of way. Sure, part of me would like to go back to being that kid who climbs trees to see a robin's nest, or plays left wing on a hockey team, or explores a school building until he gets stuck and has to wait until the janitor finds him to let the kid out of the room he got himself locked in, then has to explain to everyone what happened and how it was all an accident and everyone is so relieved that they all go to McDonald's for dinner.

She watches me for a while, then she starts talking.

"Your father loved this place, you know. He was a city boy who never had a cottage or spent any time in the country. The first time he came here it was obvious he'd found a place he loved. He'd start each day by jumping off the dock and swimming way,

way out. Then he'd spend half the day in the woods, coming back to tell me about all the birds and animals and flowers he'd seen. We came every summer, right up until Emm came along and he started to fade."

I picture him swimming with his green—always green—swim trunks. He stroked slowly, but he could hold his breath and swim two lengths of a pool underwater. He loved a high diving board and playing find-the-quarter at the bottom of the pool. He took me to every swim lesson I ever had.

"It's too bad we didn't come here more often, with you two. He wasn't good on long trips or with lots of people anymore. Not the last few years. But he loved this place. It would have been nice to have come here all together one last time."

She has wrinkles now, at the corners of her eyes, and half-circles beneath them. Grey patches have started to streak the blonde hair that she hasn't cut since he left us. There are brown spots on the back of her hands. She puts her head through the window and kisses me on the brow. I let her because it makes her feel nice. I know she's worried, and I know she's trying hard to give me space. Like I asked.

She wants me to work this out. I want me to work this out. Find some peace with his memory, then she can worry about me less, especially when she has everything else to worry about. I know I'm being selfish, but I can't help the way I feel. I'm trying to work through my feelings too. One at a time, like Dr. Nygaard said.

"I'll see you later," she says, sadly, then walks up the gravel road toward the beach. But then she stops and shouts back at me, "I'm going for a walk, then I'm helping with dinner. Do you want to come with me? We can go through the woods and see what kind of birds are here."

I shake my head one last time, and she starts back down the dirt road. I know what she's trying to do, although she wouldn't know a starling from a piper. But she knows I liked that stuff with him. She's trying.

She calls over her shoulder, "There's a talent show tonight. Emm's in it. Should be fun." She waves as she disappears into the trees.

Dad never mentioned the Camp to me, but it makes sense he would have liked it here. He loved the outdoors, the water, forests. He lived for outside. It was people he could take or leave. All the trees and birds and wildlife and the lake. I believe her. This would've been his kind of place.

Sitting in a car at the lake is not what he would have done. He'd be the first one in the water, the first to play golf, first in line to go frog hunting. He'd have dragged me out with him. No way would he let me sit here and mope, or whatever I'm doing. We'd be up in the woods looking for chipmunk nests or bear poop. We'd walk along, and he'd stop suddenly, grab my arm, and pull me behind a tree with him to point out a white-tailed deer eating raspberries or something. He'd tell me how old it was, what it liked to eat, where it was probably going. He'd show me the mushrooms you could eat to survive, the ones not to eat, the branches weighed down by nests, and the blues and purples in a jay's wing.

I pull out his pocketknife and look at his initials engraved on the handle. A couple of weeks after, I went into the garage and searched until I found it. I didn't tell Mom or Emm, but I've carried it with me ever since. It reminds me of the first time we went overnight camping together. "It's good to have a pocketknife with you," he said as he trimmed some branches for extra tent stakes. "You never know when you'll need a little help." He didn't mean the kind of help I could use right now.

I start to trace the letters when—

BAM!

I look up in fright.

BAM! BAM!

"Ya weirdo! What're ya doing in there anyway? Looking at girlie magazines?"

BAM!

After my heart starts beating again, I put the knife back in my pocket and breathe in through my nose and out through my mouth a few times. Outside the car is this red-faced kid pounding on the back window. He's got a bucket of berries beside him. He's chubby and has a band-aid stuck across his forehead. There's a glint in his eye I recognize from the schoolyard: pure predator.

I've dealt with his kind before, on every team, in every school, under every rock. There was a kid who wouldn't leave me alone one year in hockey, on my own team. Every opportunity, he'd give me a shove or whack me with his stick, or call me names, and try to get the others to join in. Classic bully stuff. The coach tried to help, but there was only so much he could do unless the idiot started a fight. I finally told Dad what was happening, and he told me that the next time it happened, stop everything, look the kid right in the eye, and he'll back down or come at you—either way it's the last move he makes. It worked, too. I did it at our next practice when he started shooting pucks at me for no reason. I stood there staring him in the eye, like Dad said. He shot a couple more pucks, then took a run at me. Everyone on the ice could see what was happening. The coaches grabbed him, and he got suspended for three games. When he came back, he didn't bug me anymore. After a few games, the coach even put us on the same line. We played okay together. By the end of the season, he invited me to his house for a sleepover. I already had other plans that weekend, or, at least, I made some.

I look this maniac right in the eye, like Dad said. I stare at him.

"What?" He shouts.

I keep staring.

He looks behind his back, then back at me "WHAT?"

This drives him crazy.

"You piece of shit!" he yells, then he starts to come around the car. I know I have him by this point, I can wait out his fury. "C'mere you little worm! Give me something to grab."

I think to myself, *really?* Does that work for him? What, am I supposed to feel sorry for him and punch myself in the nose?

"I betcha think you're safe 'cuz you're locked in a car? Well, you're not!"

He reaches through the half-open window. His fingertip brushes against my shoulder, so I quickly move further into the recesses of the car. I notice the button to lock the door is brushing against his arm, but underneath it is the crank to roll the window. He could pop open the lock and crawl inside after me, but he's either not thinking clearly 'cuz I pissed him off, or he is as stupid as he looks. I lean forward, toward him—which surprises him, and he flinches backwards—then I start to roll up the window his arm is reaching through.

"What're ya doing? Don't do that! Don't do that!"

He isn't the brightest bulb on the planet. As the window goes up so does his arm. Eventually, I get it high enough that he no longer can reach the lock button. I'm not sure it even occurred to him. I shake my head and grin at him.

"What? What're you shaking your head at? You're the retard that won't get out of the car! What's wrong with you anyway? What're you afraid of, sitting in there? You an idiot?"

"Me?" I say, with maybe with too much of a smirk.

Well, that does it. The moron starts waving his arm through the small space I've left open and starts throwing himself against the car yelling, "You calling me an idiot? You know who I am? I'm gonna rip your throat out! I'm gonna kick you in the balls! C'mere, you little snot!"

His face is beet red. He's worked up and his spit splatters the window. He's stomping a foot against the side of Mom's car.

I wonder if he might have rabies like Old Yeller.

I'm also thinking: Where the hell is everybody?

I start to roll the window up more and more.

"Hey! Stop that! You can't close the window on my arm!"

I keep slowly closing the window, but I am worried he'll be too stupid or too stubborn to move his arm, and I'll end up hurting him. I keep cranking, and the window keeps closing. When his arm starts to get squeezed, even he has sense enough to pull it free. I finish rolling it all the way up.

You'd think a closed window and a locked door would mean it's over. But this guy stands outside the car glaring at me. His fists are clenched, his eyes have that deranged look, his shoulders heave. He's looking around, and it's almost as if I can see him thinking, but he seems unable to figure out another line of attack.

BAM! BAM!

He slaps the car window a few more times, but when I don't even look up, he gives up and shouts, "You're dead, dickhead! I'll be back." Out of the corner of my eye I see him give me the finger; then he stomps away into the forest carrying that bucket of berries.

Mom's idea of a walk through the woods sounds a whole lot nicer than waiting for some crazy kid to come back. But, once again, I haven't given her enough credit.

RULE #1

I.

I was floating, alone, on my back near the shore, when this kid sprinted the length of the dock, jumped, and tucked over me into the lake. The splash swamped me, sending water up my nose and down my throat. After I finished gagging, I see this skinny kid in cut-off jeans crawl up onto the big rock at the edge of the water and squat there, looking at me.

"You need any help?" he asked, like it was somehow my fault I'd swallowed half the lake.

"What's the big idea? You coulda drowned me," I said.

"Maybe you should learn to swim."

Before I had a chance to answer, the kid jumped off the rock and started bashing through the water toward the floating platform in the middle of the bay. He wasn't doing any stroke I recognized.

I watched him for a few seconds, then did my best after-school-swim-lessons front crawl out to the float. When I got there, I pulled myself up onto the platform using the handrail. There were some kids across the water playing football on the beach. I made goggles with my hands to block the glare of the sun off the water and watched their game for a few plays while I dripped on the float's grey-green indoor-outdoor carpet.

"Hey princess," the kid said. "How about sitting down or something? You're blocking the sun."

When I turned to respond, he was lying on his back, eyes closed. His legs had more bruises, cuts, scrapes, and nicks than I'd gotten in my whole life. A band-aid clung, only just, to his right knee. The nail of his left second toe was missing, and the skin, where the nail should have been, was black. There was a big bruise under one eye and his left arm had a half-peeled-off spider tattoo.

Without answering, I moved as far from him as the float would allow. The kid opened his eyes and raised himself onto his elbows.

"I don't bite, ya know."

I nodded. I didn't have the nerve to say anything.

He asked, "What's your name?"

"Anne," I answered.

"Jamie." He nodded.

"Jamie?"

"It's short for Jamie-Lynn. My mom likes country music names."

"You're a *girl*?" I couldn't help myself.

"What's that supposed to mean?"

Then I said something stupid. "I thought you were a boy."

She jumped up, red faced, and stepped toward me. I panicked, stepped backwards, forgetting I was already at the edge of the platform, lost my footing, grabbed for the handrail, missed, and banged against it instead as I fell into the lake.

"Oh, for God's sake!" she said as I came up to the surface. She grabbed my arm and helped me back up onto the float. "That musta hurt?"

I nodded, but lay there on my back, heart racing. An intense pressure that started inside my skull and came out my nose told me where I had hit the rail. I felt something dribble down my top lip and sat up. When I wiped at it, my fingers came away streaked red.

"Jeez. You're a bleeder. Here." She reached into her pocket and offered me a filthy-looking rag. "Use this on your nose."

Even though I was grossed out, I took it and wiped my nose.

"No." She shook her head, grabbing the rag out of my hand.

I stopped and braced for whatever was next.

"Hold it to your nose and tilt your head back. It'll stop the bleeding faster."

I didn't need to ask her how she knew that.

She sat down beside me, tilted my head back, and demonstrated how I was supposed to hold the rag. I held it to my nose like she wanted and tried to ignore the throbbing between my eyes.

"Look, I'd appreciate it if you didn't tell anyone about this," she said quietly.

"Why would I tell anyone that I slipped off the float and bloodied my nose?"

"If you go back in there with a busted nose, I am going to get the third degree."

"Why?" I was dazed with pain and confusion.

"Because of the old double standard. Steve Horner gave kids a black eye in two different fights. The school principal says, 'Boys will be boys!' and he gets shooed off to the soccer field. When I don't back down from some idiot on the playground, I get hauled into the office and forced to listen about how girls play with dolls and have tea parties and draw pictures of unicorns and don't fight, blah blah blah. They made me promise not to get into anymore 'incidents' or they'll make me talk to a counsellor."

"What's that got to do with me slipping?"

"If you show up with me and a bleeding nose, I am going to have to explain that it wasn't me, and I'd rather not have to."

I pulled the rag away and asked, "What's wrong with dolls and tea parties?"

"Puhleez!" She pointed to the rag. "Keep it on your nose."

I put the rag back but asked, "You don't like tea parties?"

"What's fun about a tea party? You gotta get dressed up and sit still and talk about people or *events* and pretend you're all interested in what the other people have to say. Totally boring. The whole time I could be climbing a tree or exploring a cave or storming a castle or—"

"You do all that?"

"All what?"

"Explore caves and climb trees and . . . the thing with castles?"

Jamie pointed to her eye, "You see that?"

I thought, how could anyone miss a bruise the size of a silver dollar?

"I got that leading the charge to takeover Freddy Rosenstein's bunker in the schoolyard. He's in Grade 10."

While we waited for me to stop bleeding, Jamie talked about how she took her first plane ride.

"My dad and me flew in a plane to get here. I ate six bags of pretzels and drank two whole cans of Coke on the flight." She looked at me like she was checking that I believed her. "It was all free. Plus, I got to watch a movie. It was a dumb cowboy movie, but still a movie. I never get to go to movies. We were supposed to drive here a week ago with my mom and brother, but my lacrosse team made the city finals."

"Lacrosse?"

"It's a sport . . . with sticks and a rubber ball and you run around with pads up top, shorts, and some of the boys wear knee pads."

"I know what lacrosse is. But you play with the boys?"

"Sure, there's girls and boys . . . well, there's only two girls in the league, but we're allowed."

"Aren't you afraid?"

"Are you kidding? The boys are mostly terrified of me, 'cuz I'm bigger'n them, plus I like to use my stick. A couple of games ago I bent the shaft of my stick keeping one guy out of our box. He got upset, turned around, smacked me in the helmet with his stick, and got a game suspension. Hah!"

I wasn't that surprised when Jamie showed me a gap in her mouth where a baby tooth had been knocked out.

A bell rang from shore. Lunch.

"Time to go back in," I said.

I handed Jamie her rag. She rinsed it off in the lake and put it back in her pocket, which grossed me out all over again.

"Always carry a towel," she said.

"A towel?"

"Rule #12 in the *Ultimate Handbook to Being a Kid*."

"In what?" I asked.

"Only the best book ever written. It shows you how to make a campfire, where to look for bird's eggs, how to build a catapult, all kinds of good stuff."

"What's Rule #1?"

"Huh?"

"You said 'carry a towel' is Rule #12. What's Rule #1?"

"'Always choose the path of adventure'. The author says there's tons of time to be boring when you get old. Based on what I can see, she's right."

I could think of a bunch of rules that would be top of my parents' list: Stay Safe, Don't Start Fights, Be Polite. But those rules were in a different kind of book.

Jamie jumped in and swam toward shore with the same formlessness she used coming out to the float. I watched her, admiring the fact that in the right person, raw determination could be almost as effective as good form.

II.

When we got back to the cottage, Jamie dried off and put on a shirt that had *What're you looking at?* printed on it. As we passed through the living room, Esme and her dad were having a tea party by the big propane heater.

Jamie whispered, "The toy horse seems to have its head stuck in the teapot."

"He's likely looking for sugar cubes," I whispered back. We both laughed.

I sat beside her when we got to the long table in the dining room. Other kids were already eating.

Bologna sandwiches, pickles, and ripple chips covered the centre of the table. A stack of plastic plates and napkins stood at one end of the food; a pile of forks and knives ignored at the other end. I took a sandwich and some chips, but passed on the pickles. Jamie took four pickles, a giant handful of chips, but no sandwich.

"Is there any mustard?" she asked.

I looked at her plate, then at her. She wasn't joking.

"Of course, dear," Auntie Jenn answered. She went into the kitchen, returning seconds later with a large jar of French's.

Jamie promptly pounded the top of the jar on the table until the lid popped, scaring the heck out of the boys yacking at the other end of the table, who now watched her. Using a bread knife, she slapped mustard on each of her pickles as if they were hot dogs. When she was done, she jammed the lid onto the jar and left the mustardy knife resting with its blade on the chip tray, excess mustard dripping onto the chips.

Then she reached for the ketchup. She tried the lid a couple of times, including pounding it on the tabletop, but she couldn't get it open. She asked for help from a passing uncle, who eventually wrestled it open and handed it back to her. She poured a large dollop beside her chips.

"Is there anything to drink?" she asked.

Almost on cue, Auntie Candace emerged from the kitchen with a tray full of milk glasses. Jamie took a glass, then a big gulp, before setting the milk beside her plate. She then grabbed a pickle, dipped a chip in the ketchup, and started eating. Before I knew it, the first pickle was gone, along with four ketchup-covered chips.

"This is great!" she said, a second, half-eaten yellow-green pickle between her fingers. "Is lunch always this good?"

Jamie chewed and told me about her new skateboard, which would have been fine, except that I kept getting full-on views of the mustard-pickle-ketchup-chip mash that was her lunch. I was so put off by what and how Jamie was eating that I didn't want my sandwich anymore. I didn't even want to be at the table. I worried a projectile of the mash might fly out of her mouth and hit me in the face.

"You are gross!" a voice called from the other end of the table.

Matt, a big kid who lived down on the beach and hung out with some of the boy cousins, waved his sandwich in the air. He had a sleeveless shirt with *Born to Run* printed on the chest and a big bandage plastered over his right eyebrow. When Jamie realized Matt's comments were directed at her, she stopped chewing and looked over at him. I wanted to duck under the table. She said nothing.

"Yeah, you," he mocked. "Pickles and mustard and chips and ketchup. What kind of lunch is that? What're you, a raccoon eating the garbage?"

Matt sat back, grinned, and looked around to see that his wit was properly appreciated by the boys at his end of the table.

Jamie took another bite of her pickle while looking right at Matt as the boys around him giggled.

"Listen, tubbo . . ." she called down the table.

Matt's grin evaporated. Any giggling stopped.

Then she pointed one of her pickles at him. "I'd rather be a raccoon than a pig. How about I make sure all the uneaten lunch gets packed in a satchel? You can take it with you and won't have to stop eating at all. I'd hate for you to lose a roll of fat or two this afternoon. You might faint from hunger on the beach. Strangers might find you, think a whale needs help, and try to drag you back into the water."

Jamie took a big bite of the pickle, winked at me, then finished telling me about her skateboard, not once looking back over at Matt. That end of the table stayed silent.

For the rest of lunch, I listened to Jamie's stories, cared nothing about how or what she ate for lunch, and tried not to look over at red-faced Matt.

III.

After lunch, we went upstairs to get changed out of our wet clothes.

"D'you take a plane here, too?" she asked, as she pulled out a clean pair of cut-off jean shorts, the kind I always wanted, but Mom wouldn't let me wear.

"I came up with my mom, my sister, and my brother. Dad had to stay at work, but he's coming next week. We stopped like ten times at antique stores, which were really people's barns or garages. Mom looked at all the junk they had. It was boring, but she gets a kick out of it, and we at least got to wander around and see some animals. My brother bought firecrackers from a place in Quebec City. I got to ride a rollercoaster by myself in Granby, and we stopped in this huge party supplies store where I could get some toys for my cat Ruby."

"Hey!" Jamie jumped up off the bed she was sitting on. "I've got a cat, too. Gus. He's missing half an ear from a fight when he was a kitten. He's an old softy now. If you scratch under his chin, he drools."

"Ruby turns ten when we get home. I'm throwing her a party. I bought a pack of gold and silver balloons 'cuz I've never seen that colour before. Good for a party, eh?" I rummaged around in my pack and held up the bag of balloons.

"They're perfect. Sounds like a good trip."

"Not as good as an airplane with free pretzels and Coke, but not terrible."

"Any horses in those barns?" she asked.

"No," I was disappointed to answer. "We saw a few sheep?"

I was about to put on my gymnastics shorts when Jamie stopped me.

"Here," Jamie held out another pair of her jean shorts. "Wear these over your swimsuit."

"For real?"

"Yeah, sure. The glitter on those shorts might scare away the animals around here."

I tried to play it cool, but I put her shorts on a little too fast for someone who didn't care.

"Grammy asked me to pick her some raspberries for dessert." I asked, "You wanna come?"

"Into the forest?"

I nodded.

"You bet. Rule #1!"

IV.

We drifted up the dirt road that led through the trees to the Forest City road. Jamie slung a grass switch at the tops of the weeds along the side of the road. I carried an ice cream bucket for berries. Overhead, tree branches grew together in an incomplete canopy. Sunbeams streamed through the gaps in the leaves, painting patches of light at our feet. In the shafts, hundreds of bugs gambolled back and forth and up and down, vying for space.

"Why do they do that?" Jamie flicked her switch at the swarming insects.

"Dad says bugs don't like being cold. They fly to the warmest spot. He says if a bug gets too cold, its wings won't work, and it falls to the ground."

"Is that true?"

I shrugged. "It's my dad. Half the time I can't tell if he's joking or not."

"That's annoying."

"I don't know. I kinda like it."

"But how do you know what's right?"

I thought for a second, then answered, "I guess I don't; it doesn't matter. I like his idea of a bug getting cold and suddenly falling out of the air, then warming up and flying off again. It makes them seem less scary."

"What's scary about a bug?"

"You know, they're all crawly and hairy and buzz in your ear. Some even bite." I shivered.

"If a bug bugs me, I squish it," Jamie replied. She whipped her switch across the trunk of a tree, making a cardinal burst from a branch a few feet above her.

Halfway up the road, we turned onto a footpath through the woods and followed until it emerged into a sunlit clearing. Green plants covered the forest floor. Butterflies danced over the plants. The place smelled like pine and damp earth. When we brushed back the tops of the plants, berries hung like red lanterns from their canes.

Like Grammy showed me, we pulled the fruit from the plant carefully, trying our best not to squish it. If berries didn't pull off easily that meant they weren't ready for picking and we left them for another day. There were plenty. The forest was quiet. We were together.

It took us more than an hour to fill the bucket.

As we picked, we traded stories. Jamie asked me, "What do you do for fun back home?"

"Like, with my friends?"

She shook her head, "No, I mean like lacrosse or hockey or woodworking. You know, hobbies."

I knew what she was asking, but given everything she did, my hobby seemed kind of lame, but it's all I had. I told her, "I sing."

"Yeah, yeah. Me too, but what activities do you do?"

"No, I mean I sing as an activity."

She looked at me, clearly not following.

"You know, I take voice lessons and do recitals and stuff."

For the first time I saw her eyes widen in surprise. "Like, in front of people?"

I nodded. "Yeah. In an auditorium."

"More than your family?"

"Sure. I was even in a play last summer and had to sing a song in front of, like, two hundred people."

"Seriously?" She had stopped picking and was looking at me as if to see if I wasn't having her on.

"It was *Annie*, and I was one of the orphan girls."

"You played Annie?"

I put my hands up and shook my head, "No, no. Not Annie. That was Jessica. She's great! I played one of the other girls in the orphanage. We had to sing and dance and jump from bed to bed."

"Man," Jamie said. "I could never do that. I used to take piano lessons, 'cuz my dad made me. I had to do a recital. On the day of the recital, I faked being sick, then tried to get invited over to my friend's house, but my parents made me go."

"I betcha it turned out okay?" I offered.

She shook her head. "Not even close. I had to wait ages until I had to go up to the front of the room. I was so nervous by the time I sat at the piano the teacher had to adjust my seat for me. She told me to take a deep breath, which I did, then I played like six notes and totally blanked."

"Oh no!"

"Yeah. I didn't know what to do. I sat there. It seemed like hours. Finally, my teacher, Ms. Allison, came over, put her hand on my shoulder and led me off the stage. I never touched the piano again. I never want to feel that helpless again. Ever."

Jamie's face was flushed. She used the heel of her hand to wipe her eye. "That was like twenty people, and I knew most of them. You get up in front of hundreds of people you don't know and sing and dance. Man . . . that's amazing!"

I was thinking of what to say to make her feel better, when something barrelled out of the trees on our left and knocked Jamie over.

"You think you're so smart, don'cha?" Matt had his knees on Jamie's back. "How about a face full of mud?"

He pressed Jamie's face into the ground. "Your lunch is disgusting. Who eats pickles and mustard?"

Jamie's legs were kicking, and she was trying to twist her shoulders to escape. Matt was bigger, and he wasn't about to let her up.

He looked right at me. I froze.

"And now I suppose you're best friends? Even after the bloody nose? Yeah, I saw it, while we were playing football. What kind of a moron makes friends with someone who pushes them off a float? Maybe I should clobber you instead?"

When Matt said that Jamie stopped struggling and lay still. I looked away. I knew a brave person would do something, try to help Jamie, or at least let Matt know what happened on the float, but I wanted to disappear. I crouched down by the bushes until I heard Matt jump up off Jamie. I ducked and covered my head with my arms. Matt disappeared into the forest shouting, "Stupid girls!"

I sat in the bushes. Couldn't move. Tried to breathe. I wanted
to run back to the cottage, find my mom. After a while, when I
was sure he was gone, I looked up.

Jamie had pushed herself up to her knees. She took a big
breath as she brushed the dirt from her hair. She stood, cleaned off
her legs and arms, then came over and pulled me up.

"You hurt?" she asked.

"Uh . . . I don't think so."

"Idiot," she said under her breath. She was remarkably calm.
Freakishly calm.

"Who was it?" she asked.

"Matt," I answered.

"The fat kid at lunch?"

I nodded. My parents told me not to call fat people fat. They
said it wasn't nice. I had the impression Jamie didn't care what
wasn't nice. To be honest, at that point, neither did I.

"He took our bucket," Jamie said, nodding her chin at the
raspberry patch.

My head snapped around. The raspberry bucket was gone. The
almost full bucket. All that time. All those berries. The way she
said it seemed like she didn't care. I could feel my face tremble.

Jamie put her hands on my shoulders. "Hang on. Don't let him
see you get upset. That's what he wants. The madder you are, the
calmer you need to be."

She peered into the forest.

"C'mon!" She waved at me to follow her.

She turned and strode into the trees after Matt.

V.

The path led into the lower woods. Here, despite it being the
middle of the afternoon, almost no sunlight reached the forest
floor. Everything was grey and ill-defined. I followed Jamie
between the trees, staying close enough to grab her shirt if I

needed to. Apart from the high-pitched thrum of a mosquito or a bird zinging by, the only sound was us walking.

"We have to be quieter," Jamie whispered. "They'll hear us from a mile away."

"Okay," I agreed, then whispered, "How?"

"What?"

"How do you be quieter?"

She turned to face me. "The *Handbook* says the Tarahumara walk the forests barefoot when they hunt."

I knew from her face what she was thinking.

"No way," I said. "I am *not* taking my shoes off to walk through a forest."

"Suit yourself," Jamie said. She kicked off her flip flops and carried them in her hand.

I kept my sandals on. Not that I felt good about this failure of solidarity. Sharp sticks, pointy rocks, and hairy bugs between my toes didn't interest me. We made our way down the path Matt had taken. The quiet around us made me nervous. I kept imagining an owl divebombing us, or a wolf emerging from behind a tree. I needed to break the silence.

"Say, do you think there's any poison ivy in here?" I asked.

"Shush!" Jamie put her finger to her lips.

She crouched down, staring ahead. I saw only trees. Suddenly, Jamie shot off through the forest. I had to run after her or be left behind. Alone. No way was I going to be alone in the woods.

It didn't feel like we were being all that quiet, but it also didn't seem like a good time to point this out. I ran as fast and as far as I could, until my lungs felt like they would be sucked up through my nose. I was about to shout for a stop when Jamie slowed and jumped up onto a big, mossy boulder.

"Up here!"

I followed her up. At the top, I lay gasping on my back. All I could do was stare up into the shimmering treetops blocking the sun. I couldn't move. It felt like hours before I could breathe normally again.

When I finally caught my breath, I asked, "What're we doing?"

"Look!" Jamie pointed into the woods. "But don't let them see you."

I turned onto my belly, then peered over the edge of the boulder. I saw the fort the boys had built. It had taken them days. They had used branches and leaves and boxes and tarps and old pieces of corrugated aluminum roofing that they had gathered around the Camp. When they'd showed it to everyone a couple of days ago, I thought it looked more like a beaver dam than a fort, but I didn't say anything. A flag with a badly drawn dragon flew from the shaft of a hockey stick planted on top of the structure. I could see boys moving in and out, including Matt, carrying our bucket.

"See that?" Jamie asked.

"You mean the fort?"

Jamie nodded.

"We aren't allowed in there," I whispered.

"Says who?"

"Matt said that since the boys built it, only boys can use it."

"He did, did he? And who's going to stop us?"

The obvious answer—all the boys—somehow didn't seem a good response, even if there were like five of them and only two of us. Instead of answering her question, I asked one of my own.

"How're we going to get in there?"

Jamie thought for a moment. "We have two options: we can wait for them to leave, or we can take them by surprise. I'm not going to sit around waiting for them to leave. So we need something to scare them away."

"Like what?"

Jamie motioned, crawled back down the side of the boulder, and then rummaged around in the grass. She held up sticks from the forest floor.

"Twigs? What good are twigs?"

"Hang on," she said, then she pulled out a Swiss Army knife.

She played hockey and lacrosse, she didn't care what she wore, she didn't close her mouth when she chewed, she told off boys twice her size, and now she pulled out a knife. Had I walked through the wardrobe?

Jamie pared the end of two larger sticks into a point, making two wooden daggers. She handed one to me as she tucked the other into the belt loop of her shorts. I did the same. I felt like a Lost Boy following Peter.

"Now, if we had shields, too . . ." she looked around.

Then I had an idea.

"Wait here!" I said and took off. It was halfway to the cottage before I realized that I was all alone in the forest. I slowed a moment, but told myself that she was waiting for me by the boulder and might get discovered any second. I didn't have time to be afraid—Rule #1!

By the time I got all the way back to the cottage, I had three jobs to do. First, I raided my brother's satchel and ransacked my party supplies. I used the hose at the side of the cottage, then went past Shayne sitting in the car to the toolshed where the garbage cans were.

VI.

I jogged through the trees back to Jamie carrying two garbage can lids in my hands and a bag over my shoulder.

"What took you so long?" Jamie asked.

I handed her the bag I was carrying. "I thought we could use these."

Jamie looked inside the bag. She grinned and pulled out a silver water balloon.

"How many of these did you make?" she whispered.

"Ten. It took me a while to fill them."

"These are great." She tested one in her palm.

"And then there's—" From my pockets I pulled out a book of matches and four of my brother's firecrackers.

There was a moment of silence as Jamie looked at my hand, then at me. Her left eyebrow arched, and one side of her mouth twisted upward into a menacing smile. She shook her head slowly, play-punched me in the arm, then pulled the stick from her belt-loop and tossed it into the forest.

"Don't need that anymore," she said.

"What do we do now?" I asked, tossing away my own dagger while trying to rein in the smile I knew had no business on the face of a cool, calculating operative.

"I have a plan, but we have to be quiet and coordinated to pull it off." She looked down. I followed her gaze to my feet. It took me only a second to kick off my sandals.

Jamie explained her plan.

"Agreed?" she asked.

She needn't have bothered.

I climbed to the top of the boulder with the bag of water balloons and sat. Jamie snuck around the perimeter of the fort until she was hidden behind a tree with a view of the door. She pulled a firecracker from her pocket, lit it with a match, looked up at me through the trees, then gave me the thumbs up. I launched the first balloon into the air as Jamie tossed the cracker at the entrance.

I don't think the boys ever figured out what was happening. Scottie was soaked before he knew enough to run. Matt sprinted toward the lake at the first firecracker. The rest of the boys ran into the woods as I tossed water balloons at them, all seemingly unaware of how few people had orchestrated the fury that descended upon them.

By the time I crawled down from my spot on top of the boulder and made my way to the fort entrance, Jamie was standing there holding the bucket high. "We got our raspberries back."

"What do we do now?"

Jamie reached up and pulled the hockey stick down from the roof of the fort. She pulled the dragon flag off, pulled the rag out of her pocket, tied it to the shaft of the stick, and planted the stick back on the roof. We put the remaining water balloons on the ground by the berry bucket, ready if any of the boys returned. For the rest of the afternoon, we read the boys' comic books, ate their chips, and made the forest ours.

When the call for supper came, we tramped back through the forest to the cottage. I carried my sandals.

Even though we explained about the stolen berries, our parents weren't impressed and made us apologize to the boys, which we did . . . sort of. I sat beside Jamie at dinner and plotted with her how I might try out for hockey next winter. Grammy asked if we were doing anything for the talent show that night.

"I know! We could do a play," Jamie said to me. "We did Shakespeare in school. You've already been in a play. I can be the director, and we can put on *Romeo and Juliet*! But, so I don't have to get up in front of anyone, we need to find a good Romeo."

When we asked him to be in our play, Connor agreed because of our ambush. He never really liked Matt and his stupid rules.

After the show, we ate marshmallows and drank hot chocolate until I felt kinda sick; then we got into pajamas. We lay in adjoining beds, up in the loft, talking and talking about what we could do the next day until Jamie's dad yelled up from the living room telling us to go to sleep.

SHAYNE: WATER BALLOONS AND BATS

I'm about halfway up the Vampire Trail with Frank and Joe Hardy when this girl in jean shorts, and a swimsuit, emerges from the forest. She looks my age, maybe a bit older. She sprints across the road, jumps over the short pipe fence at the edge of the lawn, and dives down the path into the cottage.

With all these kids running out of the forest, it's tempting to see what's in there. It must be more than trees, or these kids wouldn't be running in and out. Dad always said the best way to find something interesting is to follow the path others do, but in the opposite direction. He said most people go in the same direction because it's easy. You're less likely to get lost or be left alone if you follow the path others have created before you. If you go in a different direction, you might get lost, but you might see things no one else has seen. That's not going to happen if you follow everyone else.

I think this attitude got Dad into trouble at the university and frustrated Mom, but it also meant he got interviewed on TV, got invited to places like Oxford and New York and Tokyo to speak, and meant he never had to wear a suit. People wanted to hear him talk about what he'd seen walking that other direction.

He walked in that direction my whole life . . . until he didn't.

After a bit, the girl comes back out of the cottage and heads over to a hose at the corner of the cottage. She fills about a dozen silver balloons with water then packs them into a big garbage bag. When she's done, she hefts the bag over her shoulder and walks up the lawn toward me. She disappears around the far side of the tool shed. When she comes back into view, she still has the bag over one shoulder, but now she also carries two garbage can lids. She jogs back into the forest.

Before I can guess what the girl with the water balloons is up to, three kids come up from the lake. There's one kid around my age and two kids that're younger. The younger two carry garbage bags, one of them staggering with his load. The biggest and the smallest kid each have big, stick-out noses and recessed chins, reminding me of a golden eagle we saw on a family trip to Yellowstone National Park. Based on their freckle-covered faces, all three are brothers, the middle one just lost out on the eagle nose.

The two smaller kids put their bags down in the middle of the lawn. The big kid doesn't help and seems slightly annoyed that they stopped. After a rest and the smallest kid saying something, they pick up their bags and carry them to the shed. The big kid goes around the shed and drags a lidless garbage can around to where the bags are, then tosses them into the garbage. He walks toward the lake.

I can't hear because the windows are still rolled up from that psycho kid. I roll down the window as the smallest kid shouts, "But what about the bat?"

By this time, the big kid is down the path to the cottage. I hear the door bang shut. Everyone around here bangs doors. Or the doors are broken.

"What bat?" I call out the window.

The kid who yelled jumps at my voice, looks through the window at me, then points to the cabin. "Grammy says there's a bat somewhere around the cabin, maybe in it! We're going to catch it."

I'm intrigued enough to ask, "How do you catch a bat?"

He shrugs. "We don't know."

"Are you sure there *is* a bat?"

"Yes." The two kids say this at basically the same time.

They do jinx because they said the same thing at the same time and then they fight over who did jinx first and then one kid gets the other kid in a headlock, and then that kid breaks free and then they're chasing and wrestling each other all over the lawn

until the small kid breaks free and sprints down toward the lake
and the other one tears after him.

And they're gone.

I don't get to hear more about the bat.

THE BAT

For like the tenth time I say, "Dylan! Come on. They're gonna let that frog go soon, and I still haven't even seen it."

But he doesn't hear me. Instead, he's staring over my shoulder.

"What's Danny doing with those bags?" he asks.

I turn to look. Danny's by the side of the cottage, all sweaty. He's dusty enough that his black Chucks are grey now. He's got two garbage bags on the ground beside him. I can tell he's up to something, but it's Danny, and I want none of it. Dylan, on the other hand, slips by me and walks toward Danny.

"What'cha doing?" Dylan shouts.

"None of your business," Danny answers. Charming as usual.

"What's in the bags?" Dylan asks.

"Nothing."

"Come on. What's in the bag?" Dylan says. Man, he can be whiney.

Danny doesn't even look at him. "Look, this isn't for little kids. Go play or something."

Fine by me, but rather than take the easy way out, Dylan engages. "Dad's making you, isn't he? Because of last night with Scottie. We heard him yelling at you."

We did, too. Dad let him have it. When Danny taunted Scottie at the dock, Dad told him to stop, but Danny kept at it until Dad's face was beet red and he yelled at him. At that point, Danny took off. Eventually Dad caught up to him, and we saw it. I'da been bawling by the time Dad was finished yelling. Not Danny. He had this big smile on his face, nodding at Dad like they'd reached an agreement. If anyone was red-faced it was Dad. Danny winked as he sauntered past us down the path into the cottage. The guy's unflappable.

Danny squats and ties the bag closed like he's got treasure in there or something. "Yeah, Dad yelled, but he gave me a chance to explain that I was motivating Scottie."

Idiot that I am, I ask, "What's motivating mean?"

"Helping," Danny says, looking right at me.

"Helping!" Dylan laughs. "You hear that, Liam? He was helping Scottie. By calling him names and making fun of him when he was trying to get up the nerve to jump off the dock for the first time. A real big help."

"C'mon, let's go," I'm trying to get us out of this.

But Danny's timing is too good. "He ended up jumping off the dock this morning, didn't he?"

"Yeah, but —" Dylan is sucked right in.

"That proves it."

"Hang on!" Dylan's getting excited now. "Whaddaya mean it proves it? Him jumping doesn't mean you did anything."

"Whatever you say. Now get outta here? You're gonna get me in trouble and then I won't get to do it." Danny hikes the bags up over his shoulders.

"Do what?" Dylan asks.

I elbow Dylan in the ribs to get him to stop, but in response he kicks me in the ankle. I almost fall over. I should go off on my own. It's obvious this is going south. Any sensible person would leave and go read a book or eat a bowl of Brussels sprouts. But do I?

Of course not.

"They asked *me* to do it, not you," Danny says, starting up the side of the cottage to the backyard.

"Can we do it, too?" Dylan asks. And just like that, he's walked right into whatever it is Danny has planned for him. It's like Dylan hasn't learned anything in the seven years he's been alive, living in our house on Brubaker.

Danny ignores him. Stupid Dylan chases right after him.

"Can we?" Dylan asks again, trailing right behind Danny.

I can see the situation getting out of hand and feel the need to jump in. Why? Well, Dylan is my younger brother. I suppose I'm trying to protect him. That, or I'm as stupid as he is.

"Danny." I holler, "Answer him, would'ja." Otherwise, he'll drive us both crazy, I think to myself.

Danny drops the bags and puts his hands on his hips, like Dad does when he's about to tell us something he thinks is important. I gotta remember to use that sometime. "You're too small to do it. If I tell you, will you go away?"

"Yes," I say.

"No!" Dylan glares at me. Then he grabs Danny's arm. "Tell us! No one ever tells us anything."

"No one tells you anything 'cuz you're useless."

I try not to laugh.

Then doofus says to Danny, "We can do lots of stuff. Yesterday, Uncle Paul let me pull the ripcord on the fishing boat motor."

I resist the urge to laugh out loud. That's the best he can come up with? Pulling a string on an old boat? Like that's an ability?

"Not bad," Danny says, deadpan. "But this is totally different. You can't even lift these bags. How're you going to catch the—"

Dylan practically stops breathing, he's so excited. "Catch what? What're ya going to catch?"

Danny smacks his forehead and says, "I didn't say catch."

It's like a bomb went off. Dylan thinks he's caught Danny out. "You did! You're going to try and catch something!" Dylan lifts a bag off the ground. "I can help. See?"

He almost falls over backwards.

"You can barely even lift it. No way can you carry it."

I want to cover my eyes, but it's like watching a car crash—or a good magician.

"Can too." Dylan stumbles forward four steps and puts the bag down. "See! And Liam can take the other one."

"Nuh uh. No way." I don't want any part of this.

"Good. Cuz the bat is all the way up in the cabin," Danny says, then he puts a hand to his mouth, like he didn't mean to say it. The guy should be in acting. He's very convincing. He really is.

"You're going to catch the bat?" Dylan practically hits dog-ears-only pitch. I don't even want to look at him. At the moment, it's embarrassing he's my brother.

"I am not going to catch the bat."

"You are! You're going to try and catch the bat Dianne saw up near the cabin."

"No, I'm not. Now give me those." Danny makes a half-assed swipe at the bag Dylan has.

Dylan eats it up. "We wanna come. Right, Liam?" He picks up the bag again.

"Uh, not really," I say distinctly.

"Look. I'm supposed to do this. Dad'll get mad if he finds out you helped."

"We won't tell!" Dylan says. "We won't say anything."

"Promise?" Danny asks.

"Not a word."

"How about you?" Danny looks at me.

"I'd rather—"

"He'll help." Dylan jumps in. "He promises, too."

It's like he thinks I'm his sidekick or something.

"Even if we don't catch the bat?" Danny asks.

"Even if. We wanna help. Oof." Dylan almost tips over from the weight of the bag.

"Don't drop them, you'll make a mess," Danny yells. He does look pissed. He likely thinks he'll get it from Dad if there's a mess.

"I'm good," Dylan answers.

He's got gumption.

"Well, be careful," Danny says. "This is why Dad wanted *me* to do this. Not two little kids."

I don't believe a word Danny says, but the bag I'm supposed to carry isn't that heavy and I kinda want to see what Danny is up to.

Dylan gets his knickers in a twist. "We're not little kids anymore. We want to do things, too." I don't point out to him that

that is exactly what a little kid would say. Instead, I lift my bag, and follow them across the gravel road. We go past the station wagon Shayne is sitting in for some reason no one's explained to me, then head up to the small cabin at the top of the lawn.

"Now what?" Dylan asks, plopping down his bag. He's all flushed and sweaty and has to grab the bottom of his shorts to get his wind back.

"They go over here." Danny, cool as a cucumber, saunters over to the toolshed.

"But the bat's in there," Dylan points to the cabin, still bent over.

"I know where the bat is. Do you want to help, or not?"

A maestro. You gotta admire it when you see it . . . if it's not you he's working.

"Okay, okay." Dylan takes a deep breath, picks his bag back up and staggers over to the shed.

"Now wait here." Danny disappears behind the shed and comes back carrying a trash can.

I start laughing when Dylan asks, "Are we catching the bat in that?"

I look over to see if he's serious.

Then he asks more questions. "Oh! Is that what we carried? Stuff for a trap?"

Unbelievable!

Danny drags the trash can over to the bags without looking at Dylan. I mean, what could he say at this point that would make it worse?

Dylan's nodding, like he's in on some secret mission and doesn't want to let anyone else know. "We're gonna to build the trap in here? That way the bat can't see the trap, right?"

"No." Danny tosses the bags in the trash can, then drags it back behind the shed. He comes back around the shed wiping his hands on his shorts and keeps going, right past us.

Dylan asks him, all indignant, "Where ya going?"

"I'm going swimming," Danny responds.

I start to laugh. He got us. You gotta keep a sense of humour around Danny. Treat it as a learning opportunity and move on.

I figure that now, at least, we can go see that frog. I turn to ask Dylan, but he's looking at the cabin and then over at the receding Danny. I assume he's about to cry or yell or something obscene.

But I'm wrong.

Instead, Dylan points to the cabin, turns, and hollers after Danny.

"But what about the bat?"

SHAYNE: THE CANDYMAN

The Doctor comes out of the cottage singing and dancing and banging on a tambourine. He walks across the grass, then skips around in circles. A line of people—kids in front, adults behind—follow him. Most of the kids are wearing hats way too big for them.

They sit in a circle on the lawn and clap and chant. They take their hats off and then they jump up and prance around their hats in a circle. Then they sit down again. They keep doing circles around their hats, and I can barely make out the words, 'candy' and 'Candyman' as the Doctor stands, gestures that they should follow him, and then does this skippy-jumpy walk up the path, around the bushes and up past the golf course into the forest. Near the end of the train of people, I notice Emm and Mom. Emm waves at me and smiles. I wave back, but she's already turned into the forest.

There were weeks when he couldn't sit still, all he wanted to do was go outside, walk in the woods, climb mountains, go for bike rides. Most of the time it was great, because stuff like that is fun. But sometimes it could be annoying, because he wouldn't leave you alone, even when you had stuff planned already—say with a friend, or a show you wanted to watch.

Then he'd say something like, "C'mon! It's a beautiful day! What's a little rain? We'll put on a jacket! Benjamin Franklin wouldn't let a snowstorm stop him."

He got a lot of mileage out of that Benjamin Franklin story with the book and the snowstorm and bringing it back because he'd borrowed it. I'm not sure that story's even true. Benjamin

Franklin was a smart guy and all, but why return a book in a snowstorm? Even if you promised it to a friend, any real friend wouldn't make you, or even expect you to return a book in a snowstorm.

Twice that I remember, he—Dad, not Benjamin Franklin— woke me up in the middle of the night to go out and search for racoons. I'm not even sure there were any. He got this idea in his head, and there we were, headlamps and plastic-coated trail-maps, trudging around the ravine across the street looking for racoon lairs. Most of the time I didn't mind when he got all excited, because it's fun hunting racoons, or looking for sapsuckers, or watching the river for beavers and muskrats. He knew how to do all of that.

But there were also weeks when he didn't want to do anything. He'd basically sit on the couch and watch TV or sit out in the back lawn and pretend to read a book. If you saw a heron or a deer walking down the street and came running through the living room to get him to come and see, he wouldn't even move. Those days, Mom and he would fight. When that happened, I'd grab Emm and take her down to the park and fling her around on the carousel or push her on the swing and pretend to send her all the way up and over the bar. No sense hanging around a house when people are yelling.

The stupid thing was, when those weeks happened, and he was sitting there, and Mom was bugging him to get up and do something— "take your pills," "let's go to the doctor," "stop drinking" —I thought she was being mean to him. I blamed Mom for getting mad at him and making him sad.

I didn't understand.

After he was gone, Mom sat us both down—me and Emm—and explained to us that he had been sick. She said his ups and downs were because of chemicals in his head. The fun dad we liked wasn't the best, because the same chemicals that made him fun also made him so he didn't even like himself.

"We didn't tell you two because we didn't want you to worry that your dad was sick. We thought the medicine would help and he was seeing a doctor. We didn't want you to feel bad about your dad."

"Bad . . . about Dad?" I asked.

"Ashamed. He was ashamed of his illness. He didn't want you two to think less of him, so we didn't tell you."

"I wouldn't have been ashamed."

"It was a bad decision."

THE CANDY TREE

"What're we doing?" Penny asked, stepping past a yellow and white toadstool stuck to the side of a tree. Ahead of her was a line of cousins and uncles and aunts following her twirling, singing grandfather through the forest.

"We're going to the candy tree," Mary Grace answered.

"The candy tree," Penny repeated. "And we get candy when we get there?"

"No," Mary Grace shook her head. "We don't get candy today. Today we sprinkle sugar on the tree branches."

"Sugar?"

"Then we dance around the tree a couple of times and the Doctor sings, and the leprechauns make us candy."

"Leprechauns?"

"You know, the little guys with pointy ears and green vests and black shoes with buckles."

"Why leprechauns?"

"The leprechauns turn the sugar into candy."

Penny dodged a couple of large tree roots. "Do we get to see the leprechauns?"

"No, they come at night. When we're asleep."

This reminded Penny of Christmas, except for one thing. "Why hats?"

"So the leprechauns don't see us coming."

"From a hat?"

"Leprechauns can't see people with hats."

"Oh," Penny thought about this for a while. They trooped by the boys' fort, then past a raspberry patch. The trees were tall here, and it was dark even in the afternoon sun. Penny would never go this deep into the woods without an adult, or at least her big brother. She hurried forward and took Mary Grace's hand.

"Why don't we use a tree near the cottage?" Penny asked.

"You can't. It's a tree only the Doctor knows. That's why he leads."

"Once we know the tree, can we sprinkle it with sugar every day and get candy?"

Mary Grace swatted at a mosquito humming around her nose. "I don't think so. The Doctor needs to be there, or it doesn't work."

"It's special sugar?"

"No." Mary Grace let go of Penny's hand. "The sugar's normal. It's the song and dance that bring the leprechauns."

A blue jay trilled over Penny's shoulder. It was hot in the woods, and the swimsuit she wore chafed her shoulders.

It all started without any warning. She'd barely had time to put on her sandals, never mind find a shirt. The Doctor came through the cottage banging on a tambourine, wearing a floppy gardening hat, and singing a song. The older cousins all jumped up and scrambled to the mirror to grab hats hanging on the hooks there and run after him. Penny did what she saw the other kids doing. She ended up in a circle on the back lawn with a train engineer's hat floating on her head. After a song about the Candyman and rainbows, they all marched into the forest.

"We're going to a tree to dance around it and sing songs and sprinkle some sugar on it?"

Mary Grace nodded as they ducked branches.

"Then we leave, and overnight leprechauns come and turn the sugar into candy?"

Mary Grace nodded again.

"But only if the Doctor leads?"

"Yep."

"Can we watch the leprechauns make the candy?"

"No." Mary Grace turned to look at her. "We're supposed to be sleeping. It's magic. If the leprechauns see you, they run away."

"What if we wear hats?"

Mary Grace paused and bent to scratch a mosquito bite on her thigh. "I don't think the hats work at night."

Penny looked down at the carpet of moss under her feet and thought about this. She had another question. "In the morning, we walk all the way back through the forest again, and we'll get some candy?"

"Right."

"Do we have to wear hats again tomorrow?"

"I don't think so. By then the candy's there."

Penny pondered the sugar, the hats, the dancing, the singing, and why leprechauns would make candy at night only to leave it out on a tree, for anyone to get. She wanted to understand all of this. "We go today, sprinkle the sugar, wear the hats, and do the dance. Then we leave and come back in the morning, and we get candy?"

"Yep."

"But only if we don't try to sneak back at night to see the leprechauns?"

"Yes! Now would you be quiet?"

Penny played with the brim of her hat and pulled on her lower lip. On the one hand, she had to trudge through the forest and wear a silly hat and do some dance and not get to see the leprechauns. On the other hand, tomorrow there would be candy, and even her mom wouldn't stop her from eating it.

"How do you know it's leprechauns?" Penny asked.

"What?" Mary Grace replied.

"If you can't see them, how does anyone know it's leprechauns? Maybe it's someone else?"

Mary Grace threw her arms up in the air. "Like who?"

"Like your mom?"

"My mom won't even let me have candy. Plus, she's afraid of the forest, especially at night."

"Well then, someone else."

Mary Grace put her hands on her plump hips. "What do you have against leprechauns?"

"Me? I've got nothing against leprechauns."

"Well, then. What's with all the questions?"

"It's because—"

"Look," Mary Grace said. "We wear a hat. We march through the forest. We sing. We dance. Sugar goes on the tree. We come back the next morning and get candy. We thank the leprechauns. What doesn't make sense?"

"Uh . . ."

"You're wrecking it with all your questions."

Mary Grace stomped off after the others.

Penny watched her go and stood for a moment in the shade of a large maple tree. The candy was nice, but she wanted to see the leprechauns, too. According to Mary Grace, she wouldn't see a leprechaun. Even with a hat on. But she could still get candy.

Penny looked ahead into the forest. The line of people was disappearing into the trees. It seemed like no one else had questions. No one else was annoying their cousin. No one else was getting left behind.

Questions were getting her left behind. Questions were annoying her cousin. Questions might result in no candy. No leprechauns *and* no candy?

She wouldn't ask any more questions. She would go along with everyone else. Get some candy.

She could do that.

"Hey!" Penny called out, scampering along the forest path after Mary Grace. "How far is that tree?"

SHAYNE: EMM

The wind's kicked up. The towels on the clothesline have started to wave back and forth. The people who followed the Doctor into the forest now hurry out of the trees, wearing their hats, looking up at the sky, and making for the cottage. Some of them are still singing, most of them are smiling. I can see Emm singing along as she comes down the path of stone tiles by the side of the cabin. She's talking to two girls. They are nodding and giggling and twirling down the path. They look happy.

Then Emm looks my way, stops, and says something to the two girls. She breaks from the group and runs toward me.

She gets to the car and knocks on the window. "Shayne. Lemme in."

"Why?"

"It's gonna rain, and I don't wanna get wet."

"Go inside the cottage," I call through the window.

"No, Shayne. Open the door."

She looks serious, so I open the door. She climbs onto the backseat, takes off her hat, and combs her fingers through her hair. Emm kneels on the backseat. Her elbows rest on the back of the bench, and she watches me in the back of the car. She doesn't say or do anything else.

A few drops hit the windshield.

"What?" I say after she kneels there not saying anything. It's kinda eerie being stared at.

"We went through the forest to the candy tree and sprinkled sugar on it!'

"What candy tree?"

"Doctor knows where it is. You sprinkle sugar on it."

"Why do you sprinkle sugar on the tree?"

"The leprechauns take the sugar and make candy."

"You've got candy?" I sit up, thinking maybe she's got some for me.

"Not now. The leprechauns make the candy tonight. Then we go get the candy tomorrow."

"In the forest?" The rain is harder now, big drops smacking against the car's roof and windows.

"Yeah. We walked through the forest. We sang songs and wore hats, so the leprechauns don't see us, and they don't know it's us who put the sugar on the tree."

"Hats?"

"Yeah, hats."

She is excited. I don't want to wreck it. I say, "You'll have to show me where this tree is, and then I can go put some sugar on it."

"You can't. Only the Doctor can."

I think to myself that the Doctor is just hosing the little kids, but Emm seems to get a kick out of the idea, so I don't say anything.

I ask, "What're you gonna do now?"

"There's gonna be a talent show. The Doctor said. Marcia and Tammy asked me to go practise with them. Uncle Patrick is coming here for the first time in like forever, and he's bringing Jack, who's our cousin and hasn't been here before. We're doing a show for them."

"And you're in it?"

"Yeah, I'm in a routine."

"What kind of routine?"

The rain is falling hard enough that I can see the drops bounce off the grass and the hood of the car. The storm envelopes the car, obscuring the cottage. The temperature drops, and the trees sway back and forth overhead. There's a distant rumble of thunder. It feels like the world is being washed away. Emm climbs over the seat, and we both sit together under a sleeping bag unzipped and opened like a blanket.

"I think we're doing a dance."

As she says this, she sits up straighter and makes this face with her mouth and eyes open wide, and her fingers spread out and her shoulders shake a little. She does this when she's excited. She did it once when we were on a plane and the lady brought her a juice, some cheezies, and apple slices. When the lady put down the plate, same reaction: open mouth, wide eyes, fingers extended, and she said, "This looks like a good snack!" The lady thought she was cute when she did that. Emm is cute, I guess.

"That sounds fun," I say.

She looks over at me, still super excited, but when she sees me, a cloud passes over her face. She puts her hands down, falls back against the gate, and asks, "What're ya doing, Shayne?"

I realize that I've ruined her excitement about the show. I didn't mean to. I did think it sounded like fun for her. But I've noticed that it's usually when I don't mean to, that I manage to ruin things, especially for people that I never want to hurt. That little ball on my chest gets heavy again.

"Nothing," I answer.

She frowns a little. "I can see that. But why?"

"Why what?"

The rain hammers down hard enough that I can't hear anything except what's in the car: Emm's breathing, the rustle of the sleeping bag. It makes the car feel like a cave, like I'm sitting in this metal cave with my sister, and we're alone in the wild, facing the elements, surviving an angry world—her and me. It's kind of nice. I move closer to her, not 'cuz I'm afraid, but 'cuz she's my sister.

"Why're you sitting in a car when we're at the lake?" I don't say anything, and she keeps talking. "There's swimming. I saw a family of ducks. You can do jumps off the dock. You can get doughnuts in the kitchen and dunk them in sugar. We play penny poker with the other kids, and Grammy'll even give you twenty pennies to start, even if you don't know how. Tomorrow we're going over to Black's—that's the store—and we're going to get root beers and chips. Then we're going to go down to the beach and have a picnic."

"That sounds like fun."

She bumps against me with her shoulder. "It *will* be fun. And you could have fun, too. But if you're still in this dumb car, you'll miss out. Like at home. I thought maybe you'd be different here."

"What do you mean different? I'm not in a car at home."

"You *know* what I mean . . . you don't come and play anymore. Maybe you don't sit in a car, but you do sit in your room, or in front of the TV. You never come to the park. You don't ever wanna skip with me, or play house, or even checkers. You didn't see me when I skateboarded down the hill, and I only tried it because you liked skateboarding, and I thought maybe we could do it together. But now you don't even go skateboarding."

"I still like skateboarding."

"No, you don't. You don't like anything."

My cheeks get warm, and I try to think how to answer her. The best I can do is, "I still like stuff. I just don't want to do it right now."

Then she does the oddest thing: she puts the palm of her hand on my forehead, like I've got a fever or something. I flinch a bit, but her hand is soft and cool and, as goofy as this sounds, it feels nice. When she takes her hand off my forehead, she pats my cheek lightly, then puts her hand under the sleeping bag and looks down at her lap. No explanation, no obvious reason. I don't get mad or anything. It sort of makes me feel better.

The rain starts to slow. Off toward the lake, there's a patch of blue sky. Emm reaches over the backseat and picks up the hat she took off getting into the car. She gets back under the sleeping bag with the hat in her hand. She sits against me twisting and untwisting the hat's tassel around her finger. The others have all gone inside. It's just Emm and me. For a moment everything except that tassel is soundless.

"Is it still Dad?"

I just about have a heart attack when she asks this. We haven't talked about him since they found him. Mom tried to talk about him when we were staying those couple of nights at Sofia's, but we were all in shock. And then it got busy, and people started coming over and we never talked about what happened. I'm sure

Emm could feel he wasn't there when we got back home, it was impossible not to. We sat beside each other on the bench at the little chapel, and she held my hand, but we didn't say anything. Even when they got us to go and talk to the counsellor together, we talked about everything but him.

"Shayne?"

"Yeah?"

"Is it?" She looks up at me. A tear trickles down her cheek. "Dad?"

My face gets even warmer. The rain is only a mizzle now and even that's stopping.

"He's not coming back, you know."

I nod.

"But at some point, can *you* come back?"

"What?" I ask, choking out the words, wiping the corner of my eye with the palm of my hand.

"Come back, Shayne. Mom won't say it, but it makes her sad that you're sitting in the car. I wanna show you stuff, but you're in here. It's dumb. We're here now, and there's a whole bunch of fun things to do. Mom says you need some time, but it's like you're punishing yourself, and you didn't even do anything wrong."

Then two girls come out of the cottage and climb on the picnic bench and shout, "Emm! Emm! Come on! Dinner, then we gotta practise!" They're jumping up and down and waving in the rain. They have tutus on over their swimsuits. I can see glitter on their faces. The bench, the chairs, the lawn, the boulders, even the stupid unicorn float that no one has picked up off the lawn all gleam from the rain and the emerging sun. I crack open the window and everything smells wet and clean and new. Outside the car, a flicker calls, then I hear it peck rapidly against something metal, maybe the roof of a cottage.

Emm looks at me and asks, "Is it okay if I go? I wanna be in the show."

"Sure. Yeah. Go have some dinner."

"You sure?"

"Yeah."

"Okay. After dinner we're going to work on our routine. Come watch me in the show, okay? Right after dishes, the show's on."

She gives me a hug.

She's a bit blurry 'cuz of my stupid tears that won't stop, but I nod as she climbs out of the car.

She runs to the picnic table, joins her two cousins, and they all three disappear into the cottage waving their arms over their head and doing crazy legs.

DINNER

"We're doing another talent show?" Dierdre asked.

Stephen, stabbing a breast of roast chicken from the platter of meat in the middle of the table, answered, "Dad's idea. For Patrick and John."

"Dad doesn't need any excuse for a show," Ronnie added.

"Remember that Christmas pageant when he put a goat on stage?" Candace called from the kitchen.

"It was a pig, not a goat," Nell corrected.

Candace peeked her head out of the kitchen. "I remember a goat. Plus, why would a pig be in a nativity scene?"

"Why would a goat?" Jerry asked.

"There's always goats in a nativity scene."

"No, there's always a donkey," Martha said.

"Oh. Then maybe it was a donkey?"

"It was a pig," Nell insisted.

The clink of utensils and sounds of chewing filled the dining room again. At the long table sat a dozen adults, the children already fed, raincoated, and shooed outside to prepare their 'acts.'

A late afternoon rain still pattered on the windows at the back of the cottage, stirring up a fresh, earthy smell that wafted through the open back door.

"There're a few potatoes left," Candace called from the kitchen. "Roasted ones."

"Yeah, bring'em out," Paula responded. "No sense wasting them."

"They won't get wasted," Nell said. "We'll freeze them and make crabcakes later."

"Crabcakes?" Stephen asked, excited. "When're we having crabcakes?"

Nell shook her head. "I didn't say we were having crabcakes, I said—"

"Yes, you did," William chimed in from the end of the table. "I definitely heard crabcakes."

Ronnie reached for the mashed potatoes and added, "Remember those crabcakes Susan Shields used to make? With the capers in them?"

"It wasn't capers, it was pickles, cut up pickles," Dierdre said.

"I'm sure it was capers," Ronnie said. "It was the first time I'd ever had them."

Ronnie pointed his fork at Stephen. "You remember her cheesecake?"

Stephen nodded. "Yeah, I remember her boy Tad ate too much cheesecake before one of our hockey games and threw up on the bench."

"Ted," Nell corrected.

"Right, Ted. He was always a favourite of yours, wasn't he Martha?"

Martha, mouth full of dinner, pointed to her chewing as an explanation for why she wasn't responding.

Jenn picked up the thread. "I remember Ted. He was the best skier on the lake."

"Other than Dierdre," Paula said, looking across the table at her sister.

"Oh, stop it." Dierdre blushed. "That was a long time ago."

"This was all a long time ago, but I bet you could still strap on a ski and carve up a wake." Ronnie wiped his mouth with a napkin.

"Whatever happened to Ted, anyway?" Martha, having finished her mouthful, asked. "I haven't seen him around in years."

The question was met with silence as the rest of the table looked down at their plates.

"What? What'd I say?"

Stephen shook his head and answered, "Ted's not in a good way."

"What? What happened?" Martha asked.

"His boy's down here for the summer, you know." Dierdre said.

"What? Who?" Nell asked. "Where?"

"Matt, the kid whose been hanging around the last few days."

"The loud, fat kid who's always getting into trouble?"

"He's not loud, Nell. And don't call him fat. He has personality," Candace said as she walked into the room from the kitchen holding a Corning Ware container of roast potatoes. "I need some room."

Paula and Jenn hurriedly moved mustards, a bottle of ketchup, and a plate of pickles from the centre of the table. Three pickles fell onto the pile of paper napkins.

"Crap," Stephen stood quickly. "They'll soak through." He grabbed the pickles off the napkins and plopped them back onto the plate.

Candace placed the potatoes in the middle of the table and walked around William to the empty seat beside him.

"Is there any gravy left?" Martha asked.

"Yep. Here you go." Paula handed the gravy boat across the table. "Might not be as hot anymore, though."

Martha dipped her fork in the gravy boat and tasted gravy that was, apparently, warm enough for her satisfaction. She grabbed two potatoes and poured gravy over them, "Matt's here, where's Ted?"

"Are you sure that Matt is Ted's kid?" Nell asked.

"Of course, I'm sure." Dierdre shot an angry glance at her oldest sister. "He's staying down on the beach with Ted's sister Josie. She told me all about it."

Martha, exasperated, asked again, "About what? I feel like I'm the only one who doesn't know what's going on."

"The kid had some issues at school after they moved to Lewisburg to get a fresh start."

"Fresh start from what?" Martha's voice moved up the register. "Honestly . . ."

"The mother ran off about a year ago," William said.

"No!" Martha said.

"Yeah," Robert chimed in. "Packed a suitcase one afternoon and disappeared. No note, nothing. Ted at work, Matt at school.

Matt comes home, and the house is empty. They call the police, and a search starts. Then Ted realizes one of the suitcases is missing along with some of her clothes."

"My God, do they know why? Or where she went?" Martha stood and began to stack the empty dinner plates.

"Was it an affair of some kind?" Paula asked.

William shook his head. "No one knows. Lou Sawyer talked with Ted a while ago. Apparently, she called once, about three or four weeks after she'd left, and asked to talk to Matt. Ted tried to talk to her, but she wouldn't say anything except to Matt. After he talked to her, all Matt said was 'She's not coming back.'"

"Jesus!" Nell shook her head. "Can you imagine?"

"How'd Ted take that?" Martha, sitting down again, asked.

Stephen shrugged. "That's why Matt's down here at the lake with Josie. Ted took it hard. Started drinking, lost his job. The kid started getting into fights at school, broke Jimmy Hartley's kid's nose, and got suspended. Lou and his wife finally stepped in and called Josie, and she agreed to bring the kid to the cottage for the summer. Ted's gone to the Searidge programme for a few weeks, and, when he's discharged, he's supposed to join them down here."

"Christ almighty," Paula swore. "Wish I'd known. I scolded the kid earlier today for fighting with the girls."

"It's okay to remind him what good behaviour is." The Doctor stepped through the door. "He needs some boundaries and people that're looking out for him."

"Make some room." Nell waved William out of the seat at the head of the table. Halfway through a bite of dinner, William grabbed his plate and stood.

"Hey, Dad," Candace asked. "Was it a pig or a goat you had up on stage that year you directed the Christmas play?"

Nell frowned. "Seriously? Does that matter right now?"

"Is there a plate?" the Doctor asked, grabbing a napkin, fork, and knife.

"You bet," Ronnie said. He jumped up and ducked into the kitchen, bringing back a clean plate and placing it in front of his father.

The Doctor scooped some mashed potatoes, took a piece of chicken and some broccoli. He made a cavity in the middle of the potatoes and poured gravy into it, creating what looked somewhat like a brown lake surrounded by snow.

"Ew," Nell winced. "I can't believe you still do that."

He looked over at his eldest daughter. "Still the best way to make sure the gravy stays put." He then cut a piece of chicken and dipped it in the gravy before popping it in his mouth. "Delicious!" he said after swallowing the mouthful.

By this time, the rain had stopped. Out the two large windows behind the Doctor, children gathered in small groups on the grass. Some twirled batons, others did cartwheels, one group tried to dance in unison. Up by the cabin, a squirrel dropped from a tree branch onto a station wagon's roof, startling the boy inside.

"I talked to Josie this afternoon," the Doctor began. "She says Matt's doing okay. She's had a few talks with him. He's still confused about where his mother went and why. And he's worried about his dad."

"I bet," William interjected.

"I told her about what happened with Finn and the rock, about the raspberries and the fort. She thanked me for letting her know and said she'd have a talk with him."

"What happened at the fort?" Stephen asked.

"I'll tell you later," Nell said.

"At the same time," the Doctor continued, "she's already seen a change in him in the few days he's been here . . . these potatoes are wonderful. Made with cream?"

"Cream cheese and milk," Paula answered. She was about to say something more, but the Doctor went on.

"He talks to her more. Tells her about his day. He's starting to help around the cottage. The boy is finding his way. This is a good place for him to do that."

"Maybe I should take some jam to their cottage?" Candace asked.

The Doctor smiled as he pushed his still full plate aside.

"No one with any sense would turn down homemade raspberry jam, dear." Candace beamed. "At the same time, I am hoping for something more from all of you, the children included. We have a chance to make a difference in this boy's life, and I don't want it squandered."

"It'd help if he'd stop being such a little shit," Nell said. "He tackled the girls and then took their—"

The Doctor put up his hand.

"I know that, all of it. He acts out and creates barriers because he doesn't know who or how to ask for help. He's still a kid. My Aunt Louisa always said—"

"Oh no. Not Aunt Louisa," Stephen moaned.

"Did you even have an Aunt Louisa?" Dierdre asked.

"Yes, I did. She lived in a third story apartment on Sherbrooke. We used to stay with her when my father got hockey tickets. In the mornings—"

"Yeah, we know," William groaned good naturedly. "Grampa'd give you a dollar and you'd go down to the deli on the street level and buy cherry cheese Danishes and coffees for everyone then pocket the dime left over."

The Doctor smiled. "So, I've told you about Louisa? Good. She was a good person. First female psychologist in Montreal. Worked inner city. She helped some tough kids. She always said, 'There are no bad kids, only bad circumstances.'"

"Is it okay if I start to clear?" Martha asked, starting to rise again.

"It can wait." The Doctor said, motioning her to sit down. "I need your attention for a minute."

Martha sat back down, unable to resist finishing her collection of dirty plates.

"I've told the children that we're having a talent show tonight for Patrick."

"Yeah," Paula started. "We heard. You remember we had one two nights ago."

"I realise that," the Doctor said, growing impatient. "I told the children it was for Patrick, and to some extent it is. He hasn't been here in years, and his boy, Jack, won't know anyone at all."

"It's a good idea, but what has that got to do with Ted's boy?" Deirdre asked.

The Doctor put up his hand. "Let me finish, please."

Recognizing their father's impatience, the table stopped what they were doing and looked at him in silence.

"Thank you. The show's also to bring Matt into the fold a little. I've talked to Finn and asked him to invite Matt to join the number he's doing with some of the other boy cousins. We went for a swim and had a talk about the stone throwing. Then I went to talk to Josie about the incident to understand Matt's behaviour better. I talked to Finn again about an hour ago, and he understood right away what Matt was feeling when I explained about Matt's mother. Finn went right down and asked Matt to join the act."

"Finn did that?" Monica, Finn's mother, asked.

"He did. His example is one we will all follow with this boy. Agreed?"

Most heads at the table nodded in agreement, but Nell asked, "What if he keeps at it? Do we leave him be?"

The Doctor shook his head. "No. As I said, he needs to be reminded when his behaviour is unacceptable, as we do with each other and all the kids here. With a gentle hand. We want him to feel welcome. As best we can, we want him to feel safe, and, as I think we all do, I want him to feel that this is a special place."

When he stopped talking, the room was quiet, apart from muffled squeals and yells of the children outside. No one moved or said anything, holding collectively the responsibility they tacitly agreed to share. The quiet was broken by the thud of boots mounting the three stairs to the open door.

"Mom!" Penny burst into the room. "Mom!"

"Yes, dear?" Paula answered, rousing herself with a shake of her head.

"There's going to be a show! Me and Esme wanna do puppets."

"Okay. And?"

Penny, suddenly noticing she was centre of attention for a tableful of adults, pressed into her mother's side. "But we don't know how to do puppets. You need to help us."

"Show me," Paula said, standing.

Penny grabbed her mother's hand, pulled her from the table, and led her out the door.

William finished his plate of food.

Martha stood with her stack of plates and started to climb out of her seat at the table.

Nell reached for the pack of cigarettes by her water glass.

Jerry, Stephen, and Ronnie placed their hands on the table in a motion to rise.

"But wait!" Candace motioned to the table, stopping everyone. She looked at the Doctor. "I never got an answer."

Taken aback, the Doctor asked, "To what, dear?"

Frowning, Candace asked, "The Christmas pageant. Was it a goat or a pig?"

SHAYNE: THE DRIVEWAY AFTER SCHOOL

After Emm leaves, I stay wrapped in my sleeping bag, reading my book, listening to drops from the trees overhead drum against the car's roof. Mom brings out a plate of chicken and potatoes, but she doesn't give me a hard time or anything. She leaves and later comes back for the empty plate. She doesn't look as worried anymore.

At the end of my book, the bad guy has caught Frank and Joe, and, like the bad guys always do, is bragging about his whole plan, because he thinks he's won. The dripping finally stops, and a breeze flows into the car through the window I cracked open. I hear a bump and then the patter of feet on the car roof over my head. Then something furry drops onto the front windshield, and I see a squirrel butt.

There was a black squirrel on our car that Thursday afternoon I came home from school and saw an ambulance in front of our house. As I got nearer to the walkway, two men came out of our garage rolling a bed with a white sheet over a bumpy log-like shape. I could see a hand poking out the side of the sheet, rigid despite the bumps in the driveway. As I moved closer to see what was happening, I saw a blue and white plastic gimp bracelet around the wrist. I still remember thinking Emm would like the bracelet because it looked just like the ones she's always making.

In my head, I see Mom running over and grabbing my arm—grabbing me hard—then pulling me to Emm's school so we can meet her before she starts home. I don't remember anything Mom said to me after she grabbed me, or how we ended up at her friend Sofia's house. We slept at Sofia's that night and a few nights after that. I had bruises on my bicep. I traced them with my finger while they lasted—a week or so. By the time they faded, we were back home.

It took a few days after we did that—went home—and he wasn't there, for it to sink in that he wasn't ever going to be there again. He wasn't on some field study, or taking a holiday, or lecturing in some other country. He wasn't anywhere and wasn't going to be anywhere.

Ever.

In our house I had nightmares about what was under that sheet and what had happened in our house. Our house where he'd watched birds and we'd camped out and hunted racoons. Our house didn't feel like home anymore.

Nothing felt like home anymore.

TALENT SHOW

I

Mary Grace, her plump cheeks flushed, storms into the living room. "It's not there. Uncle Patrick's almost here, and it's not there." A headband corrals her brown curls. Her silver leotard does not quite flatten the roll of baby fat at her waist.

"Did you check the kitchen?" Deirdre asks, through straight pins pressed between her lips, her attention focussed on the hem of her other daughter's cheerleader skirt.

"Candace said to look in Uncle Stephen's room."

"Go look in Stephen's room."

"Which one's Stephen's room?"

"In the corner." Deirdre points to one of the three red wooden doors with *M-B* carved in them. "Try near the bed, he uses the flashlight at night so he doesn't wake everyone up when he goes to the bathroom or makes a snack." She slides a pin into the skirt's hem.

Mary Grace pushes through the red door into a single bedroom crowded with books, mugs, boots, hats, and two large guitar cases. After checking on the bed, under the pillows and through the dresser standing against wall of the cottage, she huffs once and crawls under the bed.

"Oh, gross," she moans to herself as several large dust bunnies touch her arm. The space is cluttered with boxes, blankets, two old shower curtains (one Donald Duck, the other Daisy), a banjo case, outdated newspapers, a white Parka, two coils of rope, and—wedged between a Time-Life coffee table book on space and a green glass Japanese fishing bubble—a flashlight. She reaches through the debris, holding her breath so as not to inhale the cloud of dust she is creating. She grabs the flashlight and squirms out from under the bed.

Mary Grace stands, shakes her arm and dusts off her legs. Looking into the face of the flashlight, she presses the switch on the side of the cylindrical handle. Nothing.

"Mom!" she cries as she pushes through the door back into the living room, "Are there any batteries?" Not getting an answer, she yells, "Mom!"

A voice from the bathroom calls, "Try the chest of drawers in the cabin."

II

"Who's Patrick again?" Aidan asks.

"Your uncle," Dianne says.

"How come I haven't met him before?"

"He's been in California. A long way from here."

"Oh," Aidan answers. "But we did a show two days ago?"

"I know, but this one's to welcome Patrick and your cousin Jack."

"How old is Jack?"

"I think he's eight. He hasn't seen a show here before. When it's your turn, you get up there and show your karate."

"Karate's not a talent show act." Aidan sits cross-legged on the concrete retaining wall. Beside him is a pile of stones that he, from time to time, flings out across the water, counting the number of skips.

"But you're good at karate."

Aidan grabs a reddish-brown stone and holds its weight in his palm. "I know I'm good at karate. But it's not for a show." He launches the stone through the air.

Dianne watches the stone fly. "You demonstrate in front of judges all the time. That's like a performance."

Aidan counts six skips. His record is eight.

"Yeah, but it's not showy. It's not singing or dancing or playing an instrument. It's not something you see on TV or a movie."

"You might," Dianne answers. "But even if you don't see it on TV, you can do it tonight."

Aidan shakes his head. "No. It's a talent show, not a do anything you know how to do show. It's not like someone's going to get up and do math or paint a picture or throw a baseball."

"They might."

"You're only trying to make me feel better."

"Well, I'm sorry, but karate is interesting. It will be something different."

"I want to be in the play." He chooses another stone and whips it out into the lake, but the conversation or the strength of his feelings ruins his form. The stone hits the surface and drops.

"It's the older kids' play. They don't have a spot for you."

Aidan sits with his arms folded and stares out at the lake.

"What if I asked them?"

"Huh?"

"I could ask them . . . to give you a part in the play. It might be a small part."

Aidan shakes his head. "No."

"No?"

"No."

"You said you wanted to be in the play."

Aidan skips another stone in a manner that makes it clear he is deliberately not looking at his mother. "If *you* asked, they'd find a part for me."

"Isn't that what—?"

"But they won't *want* me in the play. They'll do it because they think they *have* to. Because an adult asked them."

Dianne puts her fingers to her temples and makes small circular movements. "Okay. Are we back to karate?"

"No. I won't do anything."

"You don't want to be in the show?"

Aidan's black eyebrows crease together. "It's only a stupid talent show. I'll do something else during the show."

He picks up the whole pile of stones and throws it, in an awkward overhand delivery, into the water.

Dianne crawls over to sit beside him. She places an arm tentatively around his shoulders. He flinches. She holds her arm in the air an inch above his neck. After a few seconds, seeing him relax, she lets her arm fall and rest on his shoulders. She dangles her legs over the edge of the concrete wall above the water.

"Did you see the frog we caught?" Aidan asks, leaning forward, peering into the water.

"Yeah. It was a big one."

"Connor said he figured out how to catch it, but it was me."

"It was?"

"Yeah. But Connor took the credit. He's in the play."

Dianne rests her cheek on the crown of Aidan's head. "I don't know if that—"

"When do I get to do things?" Aidan bangs his heel against the concrete. "How long till I get to lead expeditions and pick teams and tell Connor what to do and have people listen to me?" He wipes at his left eye with the back of his hand.

Dianne takes a breath deep breath and shakes her head gently. "Hey kiddo. I hear ya. Did I ever tell you the time when I was little—"

"Aidan!" a voice calls from behind them. Jamie jogs around the corner of the cottage. "There you are. Come on. We need you."

"Me?" Aidan shrugs off his mother's arm.

"Yes. You." Jamie puts her hands on her hips. "Unless you'd prefer we ask Scottie?"

He leaps up. "No. I'm in."

"Well, come on then." Jamie turns back up the path to the back lawn.

"What do I get to do?" Aidan calls, dashing after her.

Dianne watches him go. Then she sits still on the edge of the wall. The water ripples in the breeze from the Point. In the distance, ducks paddle around the swimming raft in the middle of the bay. She closes her eyes and listens to the lake. At the sound of a motorboat driving by, her eyes flutter open. She is about to push herself back up to standing when she notices a single, flat, white stone resting on the retaining wall. Picking it up, she tests the heft of the stone before tossing it in the air, catching it and flinging it across the surface of the water. She watches it skip and skip and skip and skip and skip.

III

"But the ribbon's come off. It needs a ribbon," Fiona pouts, holding up a silver baton.

"But, dear, there are no ribbons. We've looked. What about some glitter?"

"Mom! You don't put glitter on a baton! You put ribbons. That twirl."

Deirdre squats down to look directly into her daughter's face. "Dear. Honeybunch. Sweetie. There are no ribbons. We are at the lake. Jack and Patrick are almost here. There's nowhere even to get ribbons."

"But—"

"Breathe."

Together they take a big breath in, then let it out. Another big breath. In. And out.

"What do I do?" Fiona asks.

"Can't you do the routine without any ribbons?"

"Without ribbons?"

"Patrick and Jack are family. It's not a competition. It's for fun."

"Fun?"

"Yes. To show what you can do."

Fiona looks down at the baton in her hand. She twirls it once and catches it. Then, imagining she is leading the Eaton's Santa Claus parade, she tosses it up in the air and twirls around, only failing to catch the baton because it collides with the blades of the fan hanging from the middle of the ceiling, crashes against the living room wall and comes to a rest on the big white couch under the mirror where all the hats hang.

"Good one."

"Oops."

"Maybe outside next time?" Deirdre suggests.

Fiona plucks the baton off the couch and runs, arms open, to her mother.

IV

"We could do magic tricks," Dylan shouts from the eighth hole. He swings a green-handled putter over his head. "Like making rabbits disappear and float and stuff?"

"Levitate," Liam answers, lining up his golf ball.

"What?"

"Not float, levitate. That's what you call it when you make objects go up in the air with magic." Liam swings his putter, strikes the ball, and watches it roll up the grass, curve around the edge to the top of the circular sandy green and drop straight down into the hole. "Yes!"

"Nice." Dylan nods.

Liam bends over to take his ball out of the hole. "One problem, though."

"With you it's always about the problems."

"What?" Liam straightens.

"All you see are the problems. 'You can't build a ship out of Jell-O; it'll dissolve when you sail it.'"

"It did."

"'You can't pick up a squirrel, it'll bite you.'"

"It did."

"'Don't draw on the walls with markers, it'll never come off.'"

"It didn't."

Dylan drops his putter on the ground and scowls at Liam. "That's not the point."

"What's the point? That I'm always right?"

"No. That you never take risks."

"It's not a risk if it won't work."

"Huh?"

"Risk means that it might work out like you want it to, or it might not."

"Well?"

"It's not that I won't take risks." Liam places his golf ball on the ninth tee box. "But I'm not wasting my energy fighting the inevitable."

"Huh?"

"You know, something that's going to happen for sure, like breaking a bone if you miss the pile of leaves jumping off a tree from too high."

"That was because of the wind. And my wrist was okay two weeks later. And that's not the point. The point is, you're no fun. You're ruining my childhood."

"How?"

"What do you mean how? Like answering my idea that we do a magic show by raising a problem."

"But—"

Dylan folds his arms over his ribcage. "See? How about some support? I'm your brother, for cryin' out loud. You should support me."

"Support you in a magic show?"

"Yeah! You can be my assistant."

"Your assistant?"

Dylan nods. "Yeah. You know, help me with the magic tricks."

Liam leans on his putter, the blade on the ground, and shrugs. "Okay. I'm in. I'll be your assistant in a magic show. Tonight, right?"

"Yeah. Tonight. For Patrick and Jack."

"Can I ask one question?"

Dylan rolls his eyes, "What? What question?"

"Do you know any magic tricks?"

Liam tees off and walks down the fairway after his rolling ball. Dylan watches him go.

V

Candace, dishes dried and put away, wanders into the dining room, where Penny and Esme sit at the table with a pair of wool socks, a large colouring book, a cardboard box full of art supplies, and a margarine container of buttons. At the end of the table stands a cardboard arch about eighteen inches high with a dish towel hanging across its face. Tissue paper flags are stuck to the top of the arch. The girls jab thread at the needle each holds.

"Lick the end of the thread," Candace offers.

"Huh?" Esme looks up at her.

"The end. Make it less floppy. It'll be easier to get the thread through. Lick it."

Penny holds her piece of thread up and flicks her tongue at it. The thread bounces away. "It doesn't work."

"Not like that. Use your lips."

"Like, kiss it?" Esme giggles. Penny covers her mouth with her hand.

"Here," Candace reaches out. "I'll show you."

Esme hands over her needle and thread. Candace takes the end of the thread, puts it in her mouth then pulls it out, pressing it with her lips. "There," she says and gives the needle and thread back. "Now try threading it through the eye."

"The eye?" Penny asks.

"The tiny loop at the end of the needle. It's called the eye."

The two girls giggle again. Candace sits down at the table. "What are you doing, anyway?"

"Making puppets," Penny answers.

"For our puppet show," Esme adds. She takes her thread and needle, closes her left eye, and sticks the thread through the needle. "I got it! That's a good trick."

Penny wets the end of her thread and tries to jab it through. On a second attempt she, too, threads her needle.

"Do you need help tying the thread?" Candace asks.

"No," Penny shakes her head. "Grammy showed us."

The girls spend the next three minutes trying to knot the thread securely to the needle. At one point, Penny drops her needle on the floor, unthreading it.

"Where'd it go?" she asks, looking down at the carpet.

Candace bends over and pushes her glasses up the bridge of her nose. "There it is. Don't move, it's right under your foot." She plucks the stray needle from the floor and hands it to Penny.

After the girls finally tie on their needles, Candace asks, "Now what?"

"We need to put on the eyes." Esme holds up a button.

"We draw on the mouth and nose, but we sew on the eyes, that way the puppets look realer," Penny explains.

Candace fingers the buttons in the margarine container. "Do you know how to sew the button on?"

Penny nods. "Yeah, we watched my mom sewing buttons on her blazer. It's easy."

Candace folds her hands together on the table. "Show me."

"Sure," Esme says. "Watch."

Each girl places a button on her sock and—Penny with her tongue sticking out—pushes the needle through the holes of the button, into the sock and back out. Miraculously, neither sticks their finger. Stifling the impulse to interfere, Candace watches them, rubbing a large red button between her fingers and thumb. Out the windows behind the girls, Candace can hear a flicker tap against someone's metal chimney. She glimpses Fiona and Deirdre, in the living room, attaching sparkly material to the cheerleader skirt Fiona wears.

"Who is in your play?" Candace asks.

"Kittens," Penny says.

"Just kittens?"

Esme says, "Kittens and ponies."

"Horses." Penny looks up from her sock.

"No." Esme shakes her head. "Not horses. Ponies. They're better."

Penny puts down her sock. "A pony is better than a horse? Have you read *Black Beauty*?"

Esme, her checks colouring, says, "Yes, I've read *Black Beauty*. It's my favourite book."

"Then why ponies?" Penny asks.

"Because they're kittens, not cats."

Penny stops, looks up at the corner of the ceiling, shrugs, then picks up her sock and starts sewing again.

"What's your play about?" Candace asks.

Esme, starting on her second button, says, "The two kittens go to a pony show, watch the ponies, and eat ice cream."

"What happens to them?"

"I told you: they watch the ponies and eat ice cream."

"It's a happy ending," Penny adds.

Through the kitchen window, Candace sees Aidan charge across the lawn brandishing a wooden sword, a red towel tied to his neck and flapping behind him.

"Done." Penny holds up her sock puppet and with it comes the tablecloth. "Oh no!"

Candace takes the puppet from Penny. She cuts the sock from the tablecloth and re-sews the button onto the sock. Penny watches, eyes wide.

"Wow! You're good! Can you draw on the nose and mouth?" Penny hands her one red and one black Sharpie.

Candace draws a red nose and black mouth on the puppet. Losing herself to the craft, she adds some spots and whiskers before handing it back to Penny.

"Do mine, too!" Esme begs.

Candace does the same to Esme's puppet. When she hands it back, the girls put the puppets on their hands and prance them around the table, practising their meows and growls.

Candace watches the girls at play. "What else can I do?"

"Else?" Esme asks.

"Maybe I could make the ponies?"

Esme pulls two cut out cardboard ponies from the box. "Already done."

"How about the ice cream?"

Penny flips the pages of the colouring book until she comes to a coloured-in picture of two ice cream cones—mint chocolate chip, if the black dots smattering the green tops are any indication.

"Is there nothing I can do?"

Penny leans over to Esme and whispers in her ear. Esme then whispers something back to Penny.

Then Esme says, "There is *something* you can do."

Candace sits up straight.

Penny points to the cardboard arch. "Can you work curtains?"

VI

Standing on the picnic table in the backyard, Jamie watches Aidan and Connor in a sword fight. Anne lies supine on a blanket spread out on the grass, her eyes closed, her arms folded over her chest. When Connor falls to the ground writhing in dramatic pain, Jamie raises her hands.

"Stop. Stop it. That's not right."

Connor sits up and asks, "What's not right?"

"Romeo gets stabbed."

"But I pretended I got stabbed. That's why I fell," Connor explains.

Jamie crosses her arms. "Well, I didn't see Paris stab you."

"Paris?" Aidan asks, tucking his sword under his red cape.

"You're Paris."

"Oh yeah."

"Anyway, I didn't see Paris stab Romeo. You've gotta act it out. The audience needs to see Romeo get stabbed, or it looks like Romeo just fell."

"How else am I supposed to show I got stabbed?"

Jamie puts a hand to her chin.

"Are you sure Romeo dies?" Anne asks.

"Yep. Everyone dies. That's the point: it's a strategy."

"Strategy?" Aidan asks.

"Where everything goes wrong. In some plays everything is happy at the end, and in others everything goes wrong. In Romeo and Juliet everything goes wrong. That's strategy."

Aidan asks, "How do I die? If Romeo's dead and Juliet's dead, who kills me?"

Jamie explains, "You go to France."

"France?"

"Yeah. You go to France and start a new city that's named after you."

"Why does he go to France?" Anne asks.

Jamie puts her hands on her head. "What's with all the questions? I didn't write the play. It probably makes sense to adults."

Anne asks, "If Paris is alive, then when I wake up, won't he explain what happened?"

"He does, but you don't care because Romeo is dead, so he stabs you."

Aidan asks, "Why would Paris stab Juliet? He loves her."

Jamie sits down on the picnic table and places her feet on the bench. "Look, we don't have a lot of time, but Paris kills Juliet because he thinks she made a deal with this Jewish guy who loaned Paris money—"

Aidan asks, "What money?"

Jamie continues, "—and she lost her handkerchief."

"What?" Connor shakes his head. "What does a handkerchief have to do with anything?"

"I don't even have a handkerchief," Anne says.

"Exactly," Jamie answers. "Paris asks you where the handkerchief he gave you is, and you don't have it, then he chokes you."

"You said I stab her," Aidan says.

"That's *after* you choke her, and she confesses she doesn't love you and only ever loved Romeo."

Aidan scratches his head. "Boy, this Shakespeare stuff's hard."

"I don't get it at all," Connor says. "Why does he choke her over a handkerchief? Is he crazy?"

"That's being in love," Jamie explains. "It makes you do crazy stuff. That's what the play is about. That's why it's famous."

"Okay," Anne says. "But why do I need this bottle?" She holds up a small blue bottle.

"You drink it to kill yourself. It's poison."

"Wait a minute," Connor interrupts. "You said she gets choked and stabbed by Paris. Now she drinks poison too?"

"She's tough," Jamie explains.

"No kidding," Aidan said. "And you said this is the best play ever?"

Jamie nods. "Yep. That's why everyone knows it. It's Shakespeare's best play and he's the best play writer."

"I thought it was a love story." Anne says.

"It is," Jamie says. "Everyone dies because they're in love."

"Well, it doesn't make any sense to me. But if you say it's a good play . . ." Aidan shrugs.

"The best!" Jamie said, "That's why we're doing it."

"And this is only the first act?" Anne asks.

"Yep," Jamie nods. "Next act Romeo stands naked and yells at a rainstorm."

Connor brushes back his hair with his hand. "But I died?"

VII

"I don't want to."

"Are you sure?"

"Yes."

"But you've practised all afternoon."

"I don't want to."

"Patrick wants to see it."

"No, he doesn't."

"What if I do it with you?"

"No."

"We're gonna roast marshmallows right after."

"So?"

"Are you sure?"

"Yes."

"They came all this way."

"I don't care. I don't want to."

"Don't be nervous."

"I'm not nervous. I don't want to."

"Okay. I will go tell the Doctor not to put you in."

"—"

"Dad! Hey Dad! He doesn't want to—"

"Wait."

SHAYNE: OTHER PEOPLE

The birch trees by the toolshed sway in the post-storm breeze, shedding rainwater. The way the branches flow back and forth and back and forth is soothing. I can hear the leaves rustle, smell the wet bark, and see two sparrows glide across the treetops.

I also can hear something happening on the lawn outside. I sit up to see four kids playing by the picnic table. Aidan, a red towel around his neck, is clacking wooden swords with his brother. They're goofing around, laughing, and play-fighting. A girl is standing on the picnic table and seems to be telling them what to do while another girl—I think it's the one from earlier with the water balloons and garbage lids—lies face-up on a blanket spread out on the ground, her arms folded over her chest. She's lying there, looking peaceful.

She reminds me that every time I lie down that little ball is on my chest. It sits there and, whether I lie on my back, or on my side or even on my stomach, the ball makes it hard to breathe. I've been trying to catch my breath for weeks. Not on that day after school, but soon after. About the time people stopped coming by our house with cards and casseroles. To be polite, I had to sit in the living room with these people I didn't know and pretend that I appreciated what they had to say, wanted to eat their stupid food, needed their pats on the back.

I never understood why those people came by to have tea after he was gone. When there was nothing they could do for him. Half of them were his so-called friends, not mine, not Mom's. When they rang the doorbell and smiled at the front door, Mom was too nice to say she was tired and wanted to be left alone, but if they were paying attention they would have known. Once they finally left, Mom said sorry, because she knows it's a pain for us, but I know it's also a pain for her. What did those people think? That we wanted them to visit? That they were helping? Did they not realize they were forcing us to re-live everything, reminding us that he was gone, making it worse?

I didn't want to listen to a bunch of people. I didn't want to sit on the sofa counting the seconds before I could go back upstairs to work on a model airplane. I didn't want store-bought apple pie, or a pep talk. I didn't want other people's memories. I didn't want comfort.

I wanted Dad.

I think all those people coming by to 'check on us' is why it was a relief to climb into the car and be us three, alone, together. We may not have talked about him, but he was there. As we built the Lego skate park in the back of the car and used the washrooms in those gross highway gas stations and ate poutine in Quebec diners and lay together on the giant motel beds, it felt, at last, like we would be okay.

For those three days in the car, it was perfect. Just us.

PATRICK

Along the potted forest road, a silver car, clearly rental, bounces. Mud splashes the side panels of the doors and the hubcaps. A small head bobs against the back window with each shift of the chassis. The evening sun cuts through low-hanging branches and glints off the car's windshield. Slowly—very slowly, considering the driver—it rolls past rock and trunk and bush down the forest road's slope. As the trees thin, lake water sheens from the gaps between cottages at the end of the road.

The car emerges from the forest into a clearing, veers right, and glides onto a patch of boggy, verdant lawn. It comes to a squelchy rest, the engine cuts as the driver's door opens. A tallish, thirty-something man dressed in khaki shorts and a red polo shirt uses one hand to pull off a pair of aviator sunglasses, the other hand to pull on an impeccably distressed pair of topsiders. He grabs his wallet from the car's dash and tucks it in his thigh pocket, then stands and surveys his surroundings, taking a deep, full-chested breath before stepping around the front of the car to the passenger's side.

The man eases open the rear door, catching the limp body of a boy in his arms. He cradles the inert weight and with his left hip taps the door closed, if not shut. He kisses the sleeping boy on the forehead, then glides down the lawn toward the brown and yellow building across the gravel road. Hefting the boy, he makes note of an empty bucket by the pipe fence that borders the back lawn, someone sitting in a station wagon parked over by the cabin, a unicorn floatie resting on a lawn chair, and a group of children on the lawn playing with swords and capes.

One of the boys asks the others, "Who's that?"

The man nods a wordless greeting, motioning with his chin to the sleeping child in his arms. They take his meaning and quiet. A girl standing on the picnic table raises a finger to her lips.

Past the picnic table and a rusty grill, he stops at the three steps to the door. Here he stands, looking at the door. The man tilts back at his waist and peers down the side of the cottage, where he sees a second, also closed, door. As he climbs the three steps, the door flies open. A curly-haired girl bounds down the steps, carrying a flashlight. She dashes up the stone path toward the cabin at the edge of the forest.

The man sticks out his left foot and the door caroms painfully off his ankle, staying open long enough for him to shuffle through and into the cottage. Past two young girls, each with a sock puppet on her hand, in the living room he is greeted by the astonished eyes of two women, one with her lips full of pins. He lifts the sleeping boy to ask where to relinquish his load. The woman without the pins stands and opens one of the swinging red doors.

He enters a cramped bedroom with an impressive assortment of blankets, shirts, lifejackets, space heaters, rolled carpets, and raincoats stuffed or hung at the foot of a double bed. He lowers the boy onto the bed, takes a quilt from the stack on a mirrored dresser and unfurls it, guiding its descent to cover the child.

He stands and watches the oblivious boy; then, as quietly as he can, given the swinging door's metal spring, the man pushes back into the living room and is embraced.

"You came," the woman without the pins says.

He looks down at the sister to whom he is closest in age if furthest in height. In their shared childhood, she was a ribbon-wearing, bully-fighting, rabbit-catching, dog-chasing, ravine-jumping, treasure-hunting, hole-digging, tree-climbing, banjo-playing companion. She smiles, and he can't help but notice the start of crow's feet at the corners of her pale, blue eyes.

"Hey, Nell," he says.

"Let me go find Mom."

"Wait a bit. I'm tired. It looks like there's something going on here."

"A talent show, for you and Jack."

He looks around the living room, littered with clothes and teacups and empty plates and sewing implements. "Mom's probably getting someone's costume ready or tuning a guitar or applying makeup."

She starts to answer, but he holds up his hand and says, "I wouldn't mind a cup of tea."

Nell drops the measuring tape and the tailor's pencil she holds onto a chair and motions him to follow. She leads him back through the cottage.

"When did he fall asleep?" she asks.

"At the border."

They move into the dining room. He pats the shoulder of a woman now sitting with the two girls and says, "Hey, Candace."

She turns toward him.

"My God!" She lunges and wraps her arms around his chest, nearly knocking him over, tears trickling down her cheeks by the time he plants a kiss on one.

"Getting a cup of tea. Interested?"

Candace shakes her head, releases him, and covers her mouth with a hand. He can feel her eyes follow him as he crosses the room.

In the kitchen, Nell has started the kettle and set two mugs on the counter. "Mom said you were coming, but she says that every year. We started to believe that maybe she was right this time when Dad suggested we organize a talent show for you and Jack."

"I wasn't sure I was coming myself," he says. "How have you been?"

"Don't change the subject." She play-punches him in the arm and picks up the kettle. "Milk, no sugar?"

He nods.

She pours.

As Nell dollops milk into the tea, the cottage door bangs open. A wrinkled, grey haired woman strides across the carpet into the kitchen, cigarette in hand, arms open wide.

In a lawn chair, surrounded by family he doesn't know, Patrick watches a nephew wiggle a spoon between two fingers, magically transforming it from stainless steel to rubber. His third mug of tea is half full but cold now, and rests under his chair on the grass. To his right, the lake spreads beyond the wooden dock. In the distance, a ski-boat speeds over its surface. Across the water is the foreign country where he lives, and which gives his son nationality. From this vantage, the other country looks no different from this one—cottages dotting the shore at irregular intervals, their brightly painted colours muted only by distance.

As the magician bows and, flush-cheeked, exits the patch of grass that acts as a stage, a group of five boys walks into the abandoned space. They are dressed in black, with sunglasses; the smallest one wears a black fedora, the largest has a bandage on his forehead. A portable tape deck is placed on the boulder behind the kids, and Deirdre presses a button. As Michael Jackson's voice pierces the air, singing the first three letters of the alphabet, the boys begin to dance in a somewhat synchronized imitation of what the famous brothers might do before thousands.

Fatigued now, it takes him a few moments to realize that one of the five is the boy he left sleeping an hour ago.

A magenta and orange sun settles into the trees on the far side of the lake as a loon, heralding the reach of night, calls from the Point. Patrick, a beer in hand, has pulled his chair up onto the concrete retaining wall and is seated at the edge of the water. He hears a familiar voice behind him.

"Can I join you?"

Patrick jumps up. "Dad. Certainly, you can. It's your place, after all."

The Doctor grabs another chair and slowly lowers himself into the seat. "Enjoy the show?"

"It's been a while since I sat through one."

"I remember you kids taking turns, years ago."

"I remember we were bribed with nickels to perform when company came."

The older man smiles. "It's quarters now."

They sit in silence until a duck lands, with a splash, beside the dock.

"I forgot about the sunsets here," Patrick says, motioning with his beer bottle at the sky.

"Different?"

"In LA they're brilliant, but artificial. Bright colours, but you know they're caused by smog. Sunsets here are softer, a paler yellow. Clear."

His father nods and takes a puff on his cigarette. "A good way to end any day. Tonight was especially grand."

"I forgot, that's all."

"Another beer?"

"I'm good. That loon and I have been watching the stars come out. In LA, we're lucky if you can find a dozen. Here, they cover you like an old blanket, make you feel small, like you're six or sixteen all over again."

His father changes the subject. "He's a good kid."

"Yeah. I know."

The older man sits up and turns toward him. "Joined right in with his cousins. Like he'd known them his whole life."

Patrick nods. "In a sense he has. Finally got to meet them. I hope he sleeps."

"Tired, eh?"

"He's a trooper." Patrick pauses. "These past few months have taken their toll on him. He needs the break as much as I do."

"He might be asleep now."

"I should probably try to sleep as well. LAX seems like weeks ago."

The older man takes a last puff on his cigarette and stubs it out on the concrete. "Well, you turn in whenever you want. No rules around here." He stands to go.

"It's been a long time. Seeing Jack with his cousins and everyone. I don't know what happened."

"How do you mean?"

"It seems like yesterday I left for Cambridge, waving goodbye to you and Mom at the airport. I remember Mom's purse. The last image I saw as I went through Security was her pink purse."

"Funny thing, time. Elastic. You pull as much as you can out of each day and then, when you let go, you feel the sting of all those years gone by."

"I should have come more often. Seen you. And Mom. This."

"No reason to worry about what could have been. Doesn't do any good."

"It's just . . . I should have."

"You came when you could."

"But I—"

"When you could. And that's okay."

"It was a choice, though."

"Choosing doesn't mean there was some other, better path. You're where you should be now."

"At the lake?"

"Home, Patrick. Home."

SHAYNE: FRESH AIR

"Shayne!"

There's a knock at the car window. I open my eyes.

"Shayne! You're coming, right?"

It's Emm. I must've fallen asleep. She has glitter on her face, is wearing a purple leotard, a tutu with gold and silver balloons tied to her waist. Her hair has a streak of pink, and she's wearing make-up. She says something, but because I'm a little groggy, I miss it.

"What?"

"The show's starting!" She's jumping up and down and up and down. Excited, but with a line of worry on her brow.

"Great," I say. I rub my eyes and peel the sleeping bag off my legs.

"You're coming, right? It's down at the lake." She is literally bouncing outside the window, knocking on it with her little fist, eyes wide, needing an answer.

I'm sure it's going to be hokey. Lots of baton twirling and skits with forgotten lines and giggling. But that's probably what he loved about this place: hokey shows and singsongs, games of kick the can, romps through the woods, bears and birds. Those were the moments that made him excited, brought a smile to his face. He wouldn't miss them for anything.

Except that he is.

Missing them.

And I suppose that's the point. In a roundabout way, that's what everyone's been trying to tell me: Dr Nygaard, Mom, even Emm. Whatever was inside him, it was bigger and stronger than what brought him joy. It took him. Made him leave us. Me. And

I'm still not sure whether that was his choice, or the choice of what had him.

Maybe I never will be certain.

But, I realize, this could be a place to start to live with that uncertainty. The Doctor's painting, the leprechauns, the frogs, the water balloons, the lake, the forest, the talent shows. It's here. Because I chose to stay in the car, I am choosing to miss what is here. But I don't want to miss it. Me missing this place won't change him. Me sitting in a car while the world goes by isn't going to bring him back.

That's done.

I realize that, as much as I loved him and loved what he showed me, I don't want to be like him.

I *can't* be like him.

I sit up and roll down the window.

"Yeah, I'm coming," I answer Emm. I give her a smile.

"Good." She claps her hands. "I've gotta go now. The show's starting, and we're the third act." She scoots down the path toward the lake, the silver and gold balloons bobbing at her waist as she goes. At the corner of the cottage she stops, turns toward me, and yells, "You promised!"

Then she's off again, out of sight.

A loon calls from the lake, and I can hear chanting. The light in the sky is fading.

I imagine his face, smiling, nodding that it's good that I go watch Emm's dance and chant with the others and listen for loons. Whatever else, he'd want that. I tell the thought of him that I miss him, even if he was screwed up or unwell. I miss him, but it's been long enough. It's time to move on.

I stack my books, pack up my sleeping bag, and climb out of the back of the station wagon over onto the seat. I sit erect on the back seat and concentrate. I focus on moving the little ball from my chest into a box I imagine is made from the strongest wood, meant to hold it tight. Then I imagine sliding the box with the ball under the car seat, where no one will find it. I'll figure out how to get rid of the box later.

I wonder why the guy in the song didn't put the box down for a while, even if he couldn't give it away. Sure, the box might be heavy and hard to deal with on your own, but it doesn't have to be carried all the time. Right now, for Emm, I need to put my box and that ball away. For Emm. And for Mom. For me, too.

I put my hand on the door handle and take two deep breaths, finally using up that extra time Mr. Burns talked about to steady myself for what's next.

I push open the car door and step onto the road in bare feet.

I close the car door behind me and walk gingerly across the gravel.

There's a loud cheer from the other side of the cottage.

The show's starting.

I walk over the cool grass, toward the cottage.

There's another cheer.

I start to run.

I hear the strum of a banjo.

I feel the wet grass on my feet.

I breathe the outside air.

I round the corner.

At last, I can see the lake.

ACKNOWLEDGEMENTS

This book would not have been possible except for the help and support of many people.

M.G. Vassanji, through the Humber School for Writers program, was kind enough to tell me to dump a loser and try this project. Elena Schacherl, Ron Ostrander, Karen Craig, JoAnn McCaig, Kerry Woodcock, Sarah Butson, Natalie Vacha, and Morgan Dick have let this text occupy some of their time in the East Village Writers Group and provide feedback on (at times very) rough drafts of what I wrote. Suzette Mayr and my fellow students in ENG 594 at the University of Calgary pushed me through the 'mushy middle,' especially Andy Lilley, who read through an earlier whole draft. My lifelong friends Jeff Kotnik and Mike Esterl added support and commentary at just the right time. Through the Alexandra Writers' Centre, Rona Altrows coaxed me, in the kindest way, toward the terrifying initial submission of this project to publishers. At the UC Press, Aritha van Herk pushed me to be more ruthless and thereby helped turn that initial submission into this book and Naomi Lewis painstakingly sought to clarify copy that would otherwise have made sense only to the author. Gowling WLG allowed me the flexibility at work that I needed to pursue this project.

Family has always been there for me. My parents, Fred and Tommie, always let me take on crazy new schemes with worry but support. My sisters, Jacquie and Kennedy, have always been good enough to put up with me, even when any other rational person might have left the room shaking their head. The whole crew at the Pat-Tom Lodge provided much of the spirit of this book.

Importantly, I need to thank, as loudly as possible without disturbing my readers, Stacy and Maura for always being there and encouraging me, as I know they always will.

Lastly, I would be remiss if I didn't acknowledge the now-departed Scoobie, who slept—warm and furry—beside me, without judgment, for hours on the couch and bed where much of this was written, at times my sole companion in a very long journey.

PREVIOUS PUBLICATIONS

Chapters of this novel, in different versions, have been published previously as short stories:

"Scottie" first appeared in *Alberta Views*, January 2018.

"The Fort" first appeared in *Prometheus Dreaming*, May 2019.

"An L" first appeared under the title "Karen" in *The Prairie Journal of Canadian Literature*, July 2019.

TIM RYAN works and plays in and around Calgary, Alberta. He lives with his wife and daughter, a bossy cat, and a curious rabbit. He is the winner of the *Alberta Views* short story contest. Tim's work has appeared in *The Write Launch*, *The Prairie Journal*, *Prometheus Dreaming*, and more. *East Grand Lake* is his first novel.

BRAVE & BRILLIANT SERIES

SERIES EDITOR:
Aritha van Herk, Professor, English, University of Calgary
ISSN 2371-7238 (PRINT) ISSN 2371-7246 (ONLINE)

Brave & Brilliant encompasses fiction, poetry, and everything in between and beyond. Bold and lively, each with its own strong and unique voice, Brave & Brilliant books entertain and engage readers with fresh and energetic approaches to storytelling and verse.